Acknowledgements

First and Foremost I thank my Creator, He who has many names. Thank you for the breath of life and gift of creativity. To all my ancestors that showed me the way to connect with my Creator, I truly appreciate the knowledge you passed down. May your souls live on. Peace!

Mom and Dad, I thank you both for the love that it took to create me. I hope I'm making you both proud of the man I'm becoming. I love you both unconditionally.

My brothers, Tyree and Angelo. Thank you for both guiding and showing me what brotherhood is all about.

My daughter, Samaiya. Words can't even express the way I feel about you. You will always be mentioned as my second savior. 11/15/08 forever changed my life. May the steps I take shape and mold a better future for you.

Now cousins, aunts, uncles, nieces, nephews, there are so many to name if I could name you all but I don't want to forget anyone so I acknowledge you all. From the Jones and Marshall family and extensions thereof.

W0006175

My day ones from Philly, MD, and Harrisburg. Awall, Face, Camonte, Mujahid, Rashad, Donnell, Rommell, Bruce, Kareem, Hakim, Mike Yoseph, Fee Skee.

Friends/associates, once again too many to name. I don't want to single anyone out so y'all know who y'all are. In the 34 years of my life I've come across a lot of individuals that I put in the category of friends and associates. The first time in 2011 I put this book out I forgot to mention a few so just know I don't want to make that mistake again. You know who y'all are. It's all love. No hate over here.

Enemies, if I have any I even acknowledge you all just for the sake of cleansing my mind to operate in love at all times. If you have the energy to even be my enemy I think you need to redirect that and put your time and energy into something more useful 'cause no man can curse who my Creator blesses.

Special shout out to Zara J. author/publisher over at University Publications. Vanna B. over at Hope Street Publishing. Tammy Capri over at Nu Class Publications. C. Flores over at Pen Pushers Publishing and Jewelze over at Red Sun Publications.

Last but not least, shout out to my predecessors, Donald Goines, Omar Tyree, Michael Baisden, and Sista Souljah. All four of y'all made me into an avid reader and gave me the courage to bring forth my own creativity.

Now if you're reading this right now I thank you for taking your time to read, I welcome you all to *Homicide City*.

Enjoy, Author T. Real, Owner of Made Man Inc.

Dedications

I dedicate this book to my brother, Angelo Marshall Sr. and cousin, Marquis Battle. Two individuals that I will always feel were taken away too soon. Also every other family member or close friend that passed away during my journey in life, I do this for you all. May y'all souls live through me. R.I.P. 'til we meet again.

Chapter 1

It was a regular night at the strip club. Liquor was flowing like it was a speakeasy and dollar bills were getting tossed around. Some people were even trying to make it rain, but in this case, it was only drizzling. In the midst of it all, you could find Erica doing a standing ovation booty clap for her customers, then switching to the typical lap dance. While in her own world, she had no idea Detective Mike Patterson was watching her. He was so pleased by the performance. He was trying to get the stripper to perform like Erica who was there for not only him, but also his female friend

"Hey sexy! What's ya name again?" Detective Patterson asked while leaning in toward the stripper's ear.

"Moca," the dancer with the chocolate complexion yelled over the loud music.

As Detective Patterson observed, Moca didn't compare to Silk-E. Anyone who would compare the two would come to the same conclusion. Silk-E had the body and the skills; Moca had the body and no performance skills. Moca thought that she could just get away with grinding and sliding up and down on her customer. This bored the hell out of Detective Patterson and his date. He even yawned at one point. When the song ended, Moca got paid. The patron and his date rolled out from the club to finish off their night of passion that was almost killed by a boring exotic dancer. Also in attendance was the C.E.O of Triple X Productions Brian "Action" Jackson. As Silk-E was doing her standing ovation with her buttocks, he was taping her on his iPhone. He wanted to approach her, but she was too busy with a customer. Instead he decided to go and talk to his buddy Benji. While walking through the crowd, he noticed that Benji had a wide range selection of females for his upcoming films but was only interested in one. After being escorted by Benji's security, he finally made it through the mayhem and found the front of Benji's office. The guard knocked stated his business and told Benji who he was accompanied with and they were granted access. As Brian entered, he noticed Benji finishing up a chat with one of his dancers. Once Benji found out Brian was there, he cut the conversation short and told the girl to come back later. He knew Brian's presence was about Dead Presidents. The short light-skinned female resembling Pinky the porno star caught the eye of Brian as she walked out.

"Yo Benji! I need her for one of my movies. Please set that up," he said enamored.

Benji and Brian had a five-year relationship based on Brian using his dancers for his movies. Benji has had the best from all over the tri-state area.

"But let me finish Benji. There's one in particular I want I know. She's something special," Brian stated getting excited as he fidgeted in his pocket, looking for his iPhone.

Benji quickly snatched the iPhone from him.

"Now... you know it's no recording the dancers unless you run it by me. I'm gone have to charge you extra for that."

"Aww come on Benji," Brian whined like a little child upon the scolding.

"No whining! The rules is the rules," Benji stated firmly.

"Okay how much Benji?" Brain asked, pouting.

"$1,500 and let me tell you why $1,000 extra. I'm charging you for not following my rules and another $500 because I know how special she is and if you want her that's how much you got to pay."

"Okay, deal! Now, how can I guarantee that she will call me after I give you $1,500?"

"C'mon now, Brian. In five years have I ever fucked you over when it came down to business with me?"

"You're right, Benji. I forgot you're one talented man when it comes to the art of persuasion."

"Indeed. I am," Benji agreed. He was always tooting his own horn.

"So when should I expect to hear from her, Benji?" Brian asked while passing him the money and his newly minted business card.

"Soon. You have to be patient with this one," he replied, "I know her very well."

"I'm a patient man when it comes to you, Benji. But I know you will deliver," Brian said shaking his hand and ending the business transaction.

* * * * *

Erica completed her last lap dance of the night quickly snatching her last $10 bill.

"Thanks, Silk-E!" the customer said excitedly as he got up adjusting his erection.

Silk-E was Erica's dancer name since she started this venture three years ago at the ripe age of eighteen. Three years later, a lot has changed for her. She has a three-year-old son named DJ, short for Dawud Jr., named after her wannabe boyfriend/baby father. Some would question Erica's lifestyle knowing what type of background she comes from. She was raised in a God-fearing home with both parents until her mother succumbed to cancer when she was sixteen. Even her father knows that's when it all started to go downhill for Erica. She ran away from home and began living with her girlfriend that's two years older than her, the same woman who introduced her to world of exotic dancing and fast money. That wasn't until after the fact that Erica caught her first weed case trying to sell for her baby father. She learned her lesson in that and got herself a cashier job working at a local Pathmark. The money was too slow for her since she liked to indulge in the world of fashion so she had to switch up her hustle. It was on ever since she started. It was perfect for her. She had the Hershey chocolate tone that everybody loved to go along with the softest skin. But it was her 6ft long legs and perfect apple round ass that got everyone's attention. She knew what drove men crazy. She had this move where she would get on her knees and move one cheek then the other one.

After adjusting her silky bra and G-string, hence the name Silk-E, she glanced at the time on the clock over the bar.

"Shit!" Erica let out. It was 2:30 a.m., and she was 30 minutes late making her important call to her god-sister Bria, who watches DJ for her on the weekends. Erica started to make her way to the dressing room, but before she could make it there her favorite customer that just entered the club stopped her in her tracks. It was Omar, 6'2", 200 lbs. all muscle, and his features reminded women of the R&B singer Tank.

"Damn Omar," she said, "I know you Diesel and all but you ain't got to grip a bitch like dat."

Omar disregarded her statement and let her go, then pulled out a knot of Benjamin's. This made Erica switch her attitude completely.

"Shit you can grip me up as hard as you want since you pulled that out!" Erica said while laughing at her own self on how fast she switched her attitude at the sight of all that money.

"Yeah I knew you would switch ya attitude, but hold up I know you not about to leave?" Omar asked.

"Depending on this call I have to make I might just have to, but let me make it first," Erica answered.

"Alright. Well go make that call," Omar said rushing her.

"Okay," Erica answered back as she walked to the dressing room to make the call she needed to make.

Trina's I'm Single Again blasted in her ear after she finished dialing Bria's phone number. Bria didn't answer. The phone rang five times then went to her voicemail. Erica decided to call once more. Same results. She didn't panic. The same situation happened once before and she went home to find Bria and DJ sound asleep, but Bria had turned her cell phone off that time and forgot to turn it back on. This time it was just ringing and going to her voicemail. Erica thought about calling again and leaving a message but she didn't. She just thought there was no reason to get bent out of shape, if something was to happen to DJ in the care of Bria's then she would have to take it out on Bria, point blank.

After contemplating if she was on her way home, she took a deep breath and made her way back upstairs to find Omar to get her some more money. She found Omar posted up at the bar sipping on his usual Grey Goose mixed with Cranberry.

"Are you ready to go the V.I.P Omar?" Erica asked.

"Hell yeah I'm ready for my one on one!" Omar answered while knocking back the rest of his drink.

Twenty minutes later after shaking her ass and giving him the hand job with lube he always wanted, she walked away with the knot he came in with. After Omar, she peeped the scene out and decided that she reached a nice quota and her night was over. So she proceeded to the dressing room, changed her clothes, and headed to see the boss of the club: Benji. On the walk to his office, Erica started to think back to when she first met Benji. He had recruited her and her friend to dance at his club. Benji was a slick talker and he knew what words to use to convince someone to make a certain move, especially if it was about money. Benji started out with pimping but that hustle fell short, so he got into the business of stripping since he was in love with women almost as much as he loved money. As she made it to the door she knocked, as he always wanted, and she announced to show who she was. As she walked in, he was doing what he loved to do most: count his money.

"Hey Benji, what's up?" Erica said as she walked in to pay Benji his money for the week. He was too distracted by his money to respond.

"Here's your $150 for the week," she said as she passed him his money.

"Thanks Silk-E. It's always a pleasure doing business," Benji said as he took the cash and put in his money drawer.

"One thing before you leave Silk-E," he stated, turning, "This producer gave me this card to hand to you. He said that he saw you in action and he said that he produces porno for this company Triple X Productions. He gave me his card to give to you. He wants to put you in his new films he has in the works".

"I don't know 'bout no porno's Benji, I mean I was looking to get out of this type of business and do something else, not dive further in."

"Look I was just passing on the info, you never know this might lead to something better you don't have to make a career out of it. Just use it as a stepping stone".

"I feel you on that, but I'm gone have to ponder on that before I do it. So, on that note, let me get out of here Benji. See you next time," Erica said while exiting out his office and heading to the parking lot. She hopped in her all black Grand Prix and drove off to her house.

About half an hour later, she pulled up at her house located in West Philadelphia on 56th and Walnut. After she parked, she decided to go to the Chinese store across the street from her house to take care of her late night cravings. While walking across the street she ran into a couple of neighborhood faces she was always seeing at this particular spot. It was Chase Money and his squad The Gwap Gang. Chase Money was an up a coming rapper and Gwap Gang was the name of his entourage. The Gwap Gang invested in various street businesses, but it was the rap game that they really wanted to take over and Chase Money was the ticket for them to get in. They formed like Vultron and if it was ever an issue Chase Money was the head he took care of all internal issues inside out the crew. Banks, Scrilla, and Paperboi was the muscle of any situation, and Stacks he was the David Ruffin out of the crew he popped up whenever he wanted but it was all love between them. They had two main goals and one was to show people that niggas could get money together and have love and loyalty between them without having a falling out. The other one was to make something out of nothing as they came from an environment that the odds of making it were stacked against them. That's why they lived by a code that they were gone get money by any means necessary so they hustled and made music.

Chase Money was 25 and the eldest of his crew, making him the natural born leader. He stood six feet tall, had brown skin, and always had a fresh shape up and cut at all times. With tattoos being a fad, he was the one that only had two to signify that he wasn't a follower. All he wanted was to represent for his crew. The tattoos were capital G's that stood for Gwap Gang. Once he got that tat, everybody in the squad followed suit to represent. He was the lead by example type and never wanted his people to make to the wrong moves to where the empire would crumble. As for females, they fell to his feet as he was laid back and controlled every situation. It was his love for music that brought this situation together between the five-man crew. Everybody considered him the best rapper out of the squad but never did he flex his ego to where someone else felt lesser than him. He made sure that everyone stayed on top of their game so they could shine as one.

Banks was the darkest out of the crew. He stood one inch lower then Chase but his swag was quite different. He stayed with a fresh cut and all but he always wanted to wear a baseball fitted. Being the one in love with fitted hats, he came up with the idea that they get their own with two G's on it to promote the squad, as seen from the one he wore tonight. He was 24 and second oldest; he was looked at as the capo of the crew and second in command. He, too, had pimpish ways with the ladies but the only thing they didn't like about him was that he was too aggressive, but he was a straight G and didn't want to change that one bit.

Scrilla was the one that always stood out being he was light-skinned with braids and had the most tattoos. He had the two G's by his right eye. No one else had the courage to get a tattoo on their face except Scrilla. They all thought the idea was hot since it represented for the squad respectively.

By the look of his tats and his demeanor, a person could tell that at any given time, he was ready to take it to the max in the streets. He was the common foot soldier but Chase didn't want him to just have a soldier's mentality since soldiers were expendable. Chase thought of his whole crew as bosses that came together so he wanted everybody to carry themselves that way. But with the mentality Scrilla kept it helped in many ways because if it went down anywhere it could be in the library he didn't care he would go out in a blaze of fire if it was to fight for his squad. He was bound by love and loyalty to the end.

Paperboi was the pretty boy out of the crew. He was light-skinned but just a tad darker than Scrilla. He stayed with a fresh cut and shape up that complemented his 360-degree waves in his hair. He was all about two things: money and the ladies. He hustled so he could get money and flash his cash for the ladies. He rapped because he knew that he could make money off of it and pull girls that way. The one thing about the 22-year-old fella was he never walked around broke, but deep down he knew that the females he dealt with didn't like broke niggas. His squad didn't hate that he could get more females than them. They actually loved it, since the females he bagged always had friends and that meant that the whole squad was getting pussy on the strength of Paperboi. One other fetish he had was jewelry, but it he kept it basic between watches and chains. On a normal day and night he donned a

G-shock with diamonds in the bezel as the one he wore at the moment, but if it was a show or some type of party he wore his presidential Rolex with the diamonds in every part of the watch. As always, it was to catch the ladies eye to make it easier to get their number. He bought a chain that everybody from the crew wore some time or another that had two G's with nothing but diamonds in them. The chains were blinding to anyone who walked into a room they were in.

Last but not least: Stacks. He was the youngest even though he and Paperboi were the same age. He was the Mozart out of the crew. He made sure that he produced the magic that his squad rapped over. He would go days cramped up in the studio making sure that every track was made to perfection. He had family all over the city that rapped but he put his all into the Gwap Gang. Since he dedicated most of his time to the studio, Chase Money didn't want him in the streets with them while they did their dirt. They knew that at any time they needed him to put in work, he would be there at the drop of a dime. As Erica walked into their presence, Chase Money was the first to speak.

"What's up, Erica? We got dubs of Kush," Chase Money said as he blew out some smoke from the Dutch they already had lit up as she walked up.

"For real? Let me get 2," Erica said as she walked inside and ordered her shrimp lo mein, Arizona tea, and 4 Dutch's. She stepped outside to get her Kush and holla at Chase Money.

"What's up, Chase Money? How's the rapping coming along?" she asked.

"Everything is official. I put up our website GwapGang.com, and I put out a Street E.P. called G.O.E.," he answered while passing off two dubs of Kush.

"What's G.O.E.?" Erica asked as she stared at everyone's shirt that had G.O.E on the front.

"Gwap Over Everything," Chase Money answered, "Now after we put that out, me and the squad started doing our own promotions/parties for the E.P. Now GwapGang.com is popping off. It's up to 5,000 downloads so far, and I even sold 1,000 ring tones. This is all independent, plus we got the best Kush in the city. We gwapped up, that's all I got to say. We getting money and niggas ain't fucking wit' us. Matter of fact, I know you got a computer, go on the website download the E.P. support a real nigga on his grind. Also if you could look out, I'm trying to perform at the club you work at if you can hook that up."

"Yeah, that's no problem. I can look into that," Erica answered.

"Cool, cause the show can be a live recording for my video that I'm putting together for my single Gwapped Up, and if you make that happen you can be the main video girl in it" he tempted her, smiling.

"Okay! I dig that Chase! If I make that happen you gone put ya girl in the video, I'm trying to make that happen. You know what? I just heard

13

that single getting played by Cosmic Kev on the Come-Up Show."

"Yeah, the boy is showing the squad a lot of love right now cause how we move, we just got to keep putting out them hits and we gone be good."

"I don't mean to cut you off Chase, but let me go get my food," Erica said, since she knew that Chinese food didn't take that long to cook. As she walked in, Paperboi, one of Chase Money's entourage, was staring at her ass.

"Aww man! I know she would be perfect for the video dog, look at all that ass," he said as everybody joined in for the light entertainment.

"How much for everything?" Erica asked as she walked back in.

"Nine dolla," the Chinese lady answered as she opened her side window to grab the money and complete the transaction.

While everybody was looking, a money green Buick Regal with tinted windows was creeping around the corner. This caught the attention of Banks.

"Yo! Heads up y'all! We got a wheel creeping around the corner like some shit bout to go down" he alerted everyone.

Right as he was finished with his statement, an arm emerged from the backseat window as it rolled down and started popping off shots. Everyone scrambled seeking cover. Before the car was out of sight, Banks, Paperboi, and Chase Money let off a couple of shots at the vehicle shattering the back window. They weren't about to be trifled with.

"I hope we hit one of them niggas," Chase yelled as he tucked his burner, "Nut ass niggas coming around making the block hot mad cause we getting money. Yo! Let's be out y'all before the nut ass cops get here and we all be in the precinct tonight."

Before they could leave, Erica came running out of the store.

"Yo? What the fuck was that all about?" she asked in a frantic state.

"Some hating ass niggas trying to make the block hot, I suppose. You know we don't even have no gunplay around this block," Chase answered. "But Erica we out before the cops run up."

"Alright Chase. Y'all be careful, and I'm gone holla at you on your website to let you know if my boss says yes about the show. I think I hear sirens so y'all need to be out" she stated as she clutched her food to her chest.

Chase Money and his squad cleared the area, and Erica proceeded across the street to her house. As she walked in, she went straight to her living room area and put her things on the coffee table, then proceeded to sit on the couch to take a breather from what just took place outside.

"Whoo," she let out as she sat down on her couch. "The drama neva' ends."

After her quick breather and rolling here first Dutch full of Kush, Erica went on to check on her little prince. As she walked upstairs, she heard the moaning.

"Oh shit", Erica muttered to herself as she walked upstairs, "That's why she didn't answer her phone! She in here fucking somebody!"

Erica crept to DJ's room to find him knocked out and planted a kiss on his forehead. She then crept out into the hallway, so she wouldn't disturb Bria's sex. But as she crept past her room, Bria yelled out a name that was familiar.

"Hold the fuck up! No! She didn't say what I just heard!" Erica said to herself as she leaned in on the door to listen in and her heart dropped. As soon as she recognized the other voice, she kicked open the door to the room and turned on the light.

"How the fuck you gone fuck ya son's babysitter, you dirty bastard?!" Erica yelled out as she lunged at her once lover and the father of their son.

He dodged her even with his pants at his ankles, and quickly pulled them up as he continued running out the room, eventually making it outside. Erica was right behind, catching up to him outside his brand new Grand Marquis.

"I should shatter ya fucking windows," Erica said in a calm voice with a sadistic grin on her face. She didn't want to make a scene because the cops were down by the Chinese restaurant at this point. Bria walked outside with her belongings to catch a ride with Dawud. Erica turned around to watch her put her things in the backseat. She wanted to punch the tramp, but knew she couldn't.

"So this is how you repay me after I put money in ya pocket you dirty whore?" Erica half-asked, half-stated, while gritting her teeth.

Before she could get any words out, Erica gave her a nice slap to her face that knocked her into the car and walked away. She wasn't about to go to jail over this.

Hitting didn't make her feel any better because she was like family, but she had to do something. She walked back inside and lit up her weed, blowing out a cloud of smoke. A tear fell from her face, not from the pain that her former lover caused, but how Bria betrayed her. She expected things like that from men, but women who didn't look out for one another, she thought, had a special place in hell reserved for them. After getting high and eating her platter of lo-mein, she pulled out the business card for Triple X Productions and took a long look at it. This was a move she had to make if she wanted to take care of DJ by herself since. From the look of things, his father wouldn't be around.

* * * * *

Four police trooper vehicles could be found at the scene on 56th and Walnut parked back to back. They were in the Chinese restaurant interviewing the store owner of what they heard and saw. People flooded the streets wanting to hear what was going on, but they themselves didn't answer to any questions holding on to the code of the streets- that no snitching was allowed even though they knew who the block belonged to and what went down. Even an old lady that was being questioned didn't have anything to say.

Before Officer Freeman walked back over across the street, he wanted to see if anybody else standing across the street knew or heard anything different. It was the same results: everybody heard the shots but no one was coming forward on the culprits of the shooting. He decided that he was wasting his breath and no one was going to come forward with the information he needed, so he left to speak with his superior.

It just so happened that his superior was one of the most notorious cops on the 18th district payroll-Sgt. Frank Moretti. By his looks alone, standing only five feet six inches tall and weighing about one hundred and sixty pounds, he wasn't an intimidating guy. It helped being connected to the biggest gang in the city. Sgt. Moretti was pissed; he'd paid some Jamaicans to do a job and they didn't handle the situation the way he wanted it. All that was collected at the scene of the shootout were bullet casings. He wanted the right results, either bodies or people hit at the scene to get his point across. Moretti wanted this block, and he was the type who wanted to assert his dominance. Power came first to him, being a cop came second.

"Sir?" Officer Freeman inquired.

T. Real

"Hey Freeman. Did they give you any info on who did this?" Moretti asked his prized pupil.

"No sir. All bullshit if you ask me. I know somebody know something," he replied.

"Well it's the code nowadays Freeman. No snitching even if you know who did something. Don't worry we gone find out who did this, and when we do we gone bury they ass under a cell."

"Alright guys- let's move out!" Moretti commanded the rest of his officers. His next destination was Studio 7, to speak to the boss of the shooters and hopefully he would run into them to congratulate them on a piss poor job.

* * * * *

Chase Money and his crew were back at their crib smoking weed and talking about the shootout that just occurred.

"Yo Chase? Who you think did it?" Scrilla asked.

Chase took a long pull before he answered.

"Well Scrilla, my nigga, that's a good question that I wish I knew the answer to. But I will tell y'all this though- we are not gone play detectives and shit trying to find out either. We gone continue to get this paper and keep it moving. We don't have time to waste on haters. Let the broke niggas hate. Whoever did that we gone find out eventually you can believe that. Now whoever don't agree on how I want us to move can speak up right now."

Everyone sat in silence.

"Good," Chase continued, "Now since we agree all we got to do is keep a close lookout for whoever it is and continue to do what it is we do and that is get this paper and come up."

After the exciting conversation and the smoking, everyone was starting to get hungry.

"Yo, dog! I'm hungry as shit right now. Who taking this trip to the chinks with me?" Banks asked.

"I will take that trip with you," Chase Money said feeling the same hunger pains.

Paperboi and Scrilla were the lazy two out of the bunch. Banks and Chase Money knew that they were either going to pass them money and give them a long list of things to get or tag along thinking they were going to come across some females.

"I might as well go. I feel like we gone come across some smuts," Scrilla said. This was typical for him.

Paperboi was stuck for a few seconds but he ended up agreeing to go since he came to the conclusion that he was going to miss out on something if he didn't tag along. Since their name was buzzing around town, they knew that had to strap up just in case something went down. Chase decided that they shouldn't make the move around the way they usually do, since they just got into the shootout, so he came to the conclusion to go to Danny Wok on 58th and Baltimore. To slim the chances of getting pulled over, they decided to take two cars instead of rolling four deep in one. Chase Money and Banks hopped in Chase's burgundy Grand Marquis and Paperboi and Scrilla hopped in his black Buick Lesabre. After stashing their burners in their compartments, they pulled off to drive to Danny Wok.

When they pulled up two guys and two girls were entering the Chinese establishment with two girls already inside. Chase Money and the squad hopped out and entered behind the people in front of them. The two females that were already inside moved to the side since they already ordered. When they moved, they were able to get a clear glance at Chase Money and Gwap Gang recognizing them.

"OMG!" one of the pretty petite females with African braids said.

"You're Chase Money right?" she asked in amazement.

"Yeah the one and only!" Chase Money answered.

"Well I just want to say that the E.P y'all got out is fire. I even got the ring tone on my phone." the girl said as she pulled out her iPhone and began to play it.

"Yo, that's what's up!" Banks and Scrilla said as they ego's went from zero to sixty.

"Yo what y'all twins?" Chase Money peeped as he was checking both of them out at the same time.

"Yes we are. My name is Kaleemah and this is my sister Karen."

"Why you got to be so Joe?" Karen said not feeling how outgoing her sister was.

"Shut up Karen! Now Chase do you mind taking a picture with your number one fan?" Kaleemah asked.

"No I don't mind at all!" Chase answered smiling from ear to ear.

"Good here Karen take a picture with my phone," Kaleemah said passing her the phone as she started to pose with Chase and the rest of the Gwap Gang.

Karen snatched the phone, rolled her eyes, and blew her breath in one motion. She took the photo and handed the phone back to her sister. Right after the group photo, Paperboi hopped in Karen's face to get her number.

"Yo what you mixed with beautiful?" he asked, trying to seem smooth.

"Dominican and black" Karen answered.

"Damn! That's a good mix. You single baby or do I have to take you from your man?" Paperboi said getting into his own mack mode.

While Paperboi had Karen's attention one of the boys that walked in before them kept taking glimpses of Chase Money. Banks peeped it before Chase did since Chase was in Kaleemah's face.

"Ayo, homie what's up with you staring at my man like that? Do have a problem?" asked Banks.

Banks statement, as usual, put everyone else on alert, as some shit was potentially about to hit the fan. Chase and Paperboi respectively tucked their new dimes in their cars then proceeded back into the store. When they made it back in the boy was making conversation with Banks.

"As a matter of fact ya boy look like the Chase I went to Overbrook with," he said.

"Yo Banks, chill. I got this," Chase said, "What's ya name homie?"

"Ryan but all my peoples call me Rizz," he replied.

Paperboi interrupted the small talk with asking everybody what they wanted from the menu.

Everyone requested four chicken wings and fried rice. Banks and Scrilla were peeping how the females, Rizz and his other homie he was with was peeping them out.

"Oh shit, Rizz from 62nd and Callowhill!"

Chase Money went into a special whistle and his squad hopped on Rizz. Banks was the first one to land a jab to his jaw that dropped Rizz to the ground as the rest of the squad started to stomp him out. Rizz's homie tried to come to his aid but he failed. Paperboi and Scrilla caught him with a few shots to his head. Then, it was a straight up free-for-all between the Gwap Gang as they stomped both of them. Chase didn't even waste his energy. He just stood back and enjoyed the battle with his arms folded like a true boss.

"Uh huh how y'all just gone jump them like that?" one of the girls that came in with Rizz asked.

"Bitch shut up!" Banks shouted while he continued to stomp Rizz and his homie.

"You dumb ass nigga what you thought I forgot what you and ya homies did to me in the ninth grade?" Chase Money asked and continued, "I don't give a fuck if it was a long time ago! Payback is a bitch ain't it?" He laughed at the spectacle.

Rizz and his homie managed to get out of the store and hop in their car driving off. They left so fast that they left their dates behind and didn't even care.

"Well since they left y'all, you two might as well roll out with us," Banks said speaking to both of the girls.

"Yeah that is fucked up how they left us like that," one girl with long weave almost hitting her ass said.

"Well baby we just separated the real from the fake, what's ya name?" Banks asked

"Porsche what do they call you?"

"My niggas call me Banks baby."

"Yeah he's Banks, and I'm Scrilla," Scrilla said joining in so he wouldn't be the only one without a female.

By this time, Chase Money and Paperboi were waiting in their cars for the rest of the crew. Chase was getting impatient so he started blowing his horn to signal it was time to roll out.

"Yo hold on dog!" Banks yelled out.

Chase Money just laughed at him and waited.

"So what's ya homie name? She all quiet," Scrilla said talking to Porsche.

"She don't got to speak for me. I got a mouth of my own, my name is Shareen."

"Damn, baby! I was just asking. What's up? Y'all coming with us? We got food, Kush, everything y'all need," Scrilla added.

Shareen and Porsche looked at each other to see if they both were in agreement to roll out. While they drove off, Chase Money peeped how Rizz and his homie were coming back to the scene with a squad car.

"Oh shit them niggas is snitches! They going back to the store, I'm glad we rolled out!" he exclaimed.

Rizz and his sidekick got pulled over on Cobbs Creek because he made a reckless turn speeding away from the plaza. He was on his way to pick up reinforcements from what transpired at Danny Wok. Due to getting pulled over, the cops something went down and they questioned Rizz and his homie. Rizz ended up snitching on Chase Money and the Gwap Gang adding more heat to what went down at the Chinese store around 56th and Spruce earlier that evening.

Chase Money and the Gang made it back, but before they could get comfortable eat and entertain their newly found company he wanted to have a quick meeting.

"Yo what's up boss man what's bothering you?" Paperboi asked not really wanting to have a meeting when his mind was on pussy.

"Look Paperboi them bitches can wait, this is important," Chase said.

"Yeah nigga, chill out. You know Chase don't be calling meetings unless he got some real shit to get off his chest," Banks added, knowing some real shit was about to come out of his mouth.

"Tonight we all can agree that two incidents happened out of our control, but look... we need to focus on the energy that we putting out. If we gone make the transition we can't take this negative energy with us cause we gone be back on the streets. I'm not saying that we got to walk around here like we got Kool-Aid in our blood but we got to be careful cause all this work we put in to make GwapGang.com work could be taking away from us with the snap of a finger".

"Yeah I feel you dog," Scrilla said.

"Me too," Banks agreed.

"Yeah me too boss man, but let's get back to the regularly scheduled program with the company we got in the other room," Paperboi said anxiously wanting to get down with the females.

"Always worrying 'bout the pussy," Chase said while chuckling about his comrade. With that, they ended the meeting.

* * * * *

Moretti walked in the restaurant entrance to Studio 7, walking past five customers with long dreads and blood shot eyes. The customers all were staring at Moretti because he stood out like a sheep in a wolf pack. Moretti knew it was because he wasn't black- he was Italian and they probably wanted to know why he was entering this type of establishment by himself. He didn't care. He was there for business and to speak to King. He just walked past them and went straight for the guard that he had to get through.

"You don't have to pat me down. Just get King," Moretti said.

"King, me don't know any King," the guard said in his broken English not recognizing Moretti as a regular.

"You don't know King? Maybe this will make you remember who he is," Moretti said as he lifted his shirt to show his 9-millimeter. This made the guard pull out his walkie-talkie and call King over the radio.

"Some man here to see you King," the guard said over the walkie-talkie.

"What man?" King asked as he came over the radio.

"It's me. Moretti," he said, snatching the radio from the guard.

"Let him in," King said as he came back over the radio.

The guard followed King's orders and led Moretti into his office. It was filled with a cloud of smoke, making it hard to see faces. Moretti coughed from the strong reefer cloud that was in the room from King and his men puffing on some Jamaican finest rolled up in white paper.

"So this is why I don't have the results I wanted huh? They too busy getting high and not doing the job right?" Moretti asked angrily.

"You come in my room passing judgment? Now I don't offer you a seat. You stand the whole time you're in my presence," King said not feeling Moretti's vibe.

"King I paid you five grand to get the job done. Don't forget who I'm connected with," Moretti said trying to throw his boss's name around.

"You Italians always throw that bumbaclot word around, who cares who you connected with? You see these men? They are my shottas," King beamed.

"You mean shooters right?" Moretti asked not understanding the term King was saying to him.

"No I said Shottas. These are my warriors. I command them, not you," King said coldly.

"Okay King. I don't want no war starting up, but you know if my boss finds out that the plans are at a standstill he's gonna be pissed. You already know he wants in on this side of town."

"Yes, I remember the conversation we had 'bout dat," King confirmed.

"Well good, King. That's all I was trying to say, but since y'all didn't do the job correctly, I will take care of business myself. Y'all enjoy the rest of y'all night," Moretti said as he went to exit out the office. As he walked out, a tall dark chocolate woman wearing a black, tight outfit, with heels on was on her way to enter.

"Have you ever fucked an Italian, baby?" Moretti asked the Jamaican beauty.

King heard Moretti's words and didn't like the disrespect one bit.

"Aye don't talk to me Queen that way! Show some respect, or I will cut your tongue out!" King scolded with sincerity.

"My bad, King! I didn't know. I just got beside myself," Moretti said. Deep down inside, he could not have cared less. He knew that if he saw her on the streets, he still would try to fuck her.

Sgt. Moretti stepped out the establishment and headed over to the precinct to finalize the paperwork for the shootout. Office Freeman was still there.

"What's up Freeman? What are you still doing here?" he asked.

"Yeah. I'm pissed we had a situation over at Danny Wok filling out the paperwork now so I can have this on the Captain's desk," he responded.

"So what happened?" Moretti asked, again probing for more information.

"I pulled over these guys that were speeding out of the plaza. When I approached the car, these guys were fucked up. Man, you know busted lips, puffy eyes. They looked like they were sparring with Mike Tyson. But anyways, I asked them what happened and they went into this story about how they just got jumped over at Danny Wok by these guys called the Gwap Gang. So they took me back to the scene and of course by the time I got back over there the culprits were gone. I tried to check the store camera the damn recorder wasn't even on for the day!"

"Wait Freeman. Did you say the Gwap Gang had something to do with it?" Moretti asked putting this incident in his mental notes.

"Yeah, that's what the victims told me the name of the crew was, but hopefully I'm saying it right."

"Don't worry about that Freeman. You got the name right. They're some punk ass crew from around where the shootout occurred."

"Are you serious Sgt? Sounds like they might know what happened on that corner. When are we gone bust they ass?"

"Oh don't worry Freeman. I'm already on top of it."

Sgt. Moretti didn't want anyone getting in his way of the plans that he had in motion. He definitely didn't want anyone knowing how much dirt he was into. As far as anybody knew, on the job he was the perfect officer and he wanted to keep it that way, even though he led a double life. Sooner or later, he knew he would have to choose which one would take over for good.

Chapter 2

Beep! Beep! Beep! Beep!

Detective Mike Patterson's alarm went off. He did the usual, lean his arm over and smack it a few times to find the snooze button and dozed back off. Five minutes later, the alarm went off again. He raised his head only to wake up this time to a major hangover.

He looked over at the Grey Goose bottle that was on his nightstand next to his bed and immediately regretted his previous activities.

"Damn. I know I couldn't have drunk that whole bottle to myself," he thought out loud to himself, turning to his side only to see the chocolate beauty that was lying beside him naked.

"Aneesa," he said calling her name while shaking her at the same time. She only responded by squirming a little. So he decided to give her a nice ass smack to fully wake her up.

"Damn, Mike. You ready for another round?" Aneesa said as she turned over on her back while opening her eyes.

"Naw ya chocolate ass gave me enough a couple of hours ago. I fuck around and have a couple of cavities fucking around with your chocolate ass."

31

"Ha," Aneesa responded as she scanned the floor for her clothes. She got up and located her thong, gathered all her belongings, and got fully dressed.

"Thank you for the night! I had fun at the strip club and the sex was great. I just wish you would have got that stripper to come with us. That would have made the night better, but even though it didn't happen, you still made me feel good," she said as she gave him a seductive good-bye hug and kiss.

"Better than ya boyfriend, I suppose," Mike said being sarcastic.

"Fuck you Mike, and on that note, I'm leaving," Aneesa responded as she left his apartment.

Mike Patterson wasn't your average detective. He was one of the youngest in the city. He lived like he wasn't even connected to the police department and it showed through his actions with the opposite sex. His fellow workers called him the GQ of detectives. He stayed with a fresh suit and a pair of Salvatore Ferragamos. He earned his position through ten years of hard work, as he started ten years ago at the age of 20. At the age of thirty, his business was square at the job. It was his personal life he couldn't get on track, mainly due to the fact that women just threw their panties at him and he rarely turned down the pussy. This behavior came between him and his baby-mother of five years. He tried living the family man's life but he couldn't keep his dick to just one woman. He didn't get raised to be this way, but it was who he was. His Father was the same way, so he knew that he was going to have the same struggle.

Getting himself together for the day, he pulled out his all black Tom Ford suit, black shirt to go under, then grabbed his favorite Salvatore Ferragamos. He then jumped in the shower, hopped out to shape up his head and goatee, brushed his teeth, got dressed, and then proceeded to the kitchen for breakfast.

"This hangover is in the way," Mike muttered to himself as he thought about what he had a taste for. He didn't want to eat the wrong thing knowing it might have him hurling all over his brand new suit and shoes. He just made some toast and coffee and then took some Tylenol to handle the headache he had. After his quick breakfast, he grabbed his badge, gun, and keys, and cell phone and proceeded out the door to start his day. After pressing the button on his key ring to shut off his alarm, he hit the other button on the ring to start up his Black Buick Luzerne. While looking around in his car he found an empty condom wrapper along with the sperm filled condom in the back seat.

"Damn, so we started inside my car I see," Mike said as he threw out the evidence.

"What the fuck you want? I'm on my way," Mike said out loud. He didn't even answer. He let it go straight to his voicemail.

"Whatever it is it can wait till I get there," he said as he drove off to the station.

As he arrived, he had to prepare for all the hate from all the officers that didn't like him for being in a higher position, how he dressed and how much pussy he got. Officer Freeman was always the first one to start off the barrage.

"Aww shit look at Mr. GQ of the Month!" Freeman teased.

"Fuck you, Freeman," Mike responded as he walked in. Moretti joined in with Freeman.

"Look at the black Serpico as he walks in all smooth. Which one of our wives you looking to fuck now Superfly?"

"I'm choosing yours next you greasy haired bastard," Mike responded to Moretti.

"Why you got to go racial?" Moretti said as he jumped in Mike's face.

"Hey! Cool it down!" Captain Morello laughed as he stepped out his office to see what all the commotion was all about was. "I'm glad you're here Patterson. When you get ready, I need to see you in my office."

"Alright boss. Let me get myself together and I will be in," Patterson offered as he went to his desk.

After checking his paper work, Detective Patterson walked to the coffee machine to get a donut along with some coffee. He accidently walked up on a sexy light-skinned officer who he thought had crush on him.

"Officer Johnson, how's your day going?" Mike asked to start a quick conversation.

"Everything's cool Patterson. It's just this coffee is too black and I need some special cream for it," Officer Johnson responded.

This caught the attention of Mike's ego and knew how to respond in this case.

"Come on. I know just where to take you and give you what you need."

He ended up taking her to a bathroom with one toilet and sink and a tiny window. As they entered, he was ready. He unzipped his pants and pulled his dick out for her and she kneeled down and went to work. Patterson grabbed a hand full of her hair as she sucked gently with her lips and tongue.

"Damn, Johnson. I ain't know it was like this," Patterson said enjoying the morning head.

She let out a moan, enjoying every suck and kiss of his dick as she continued.

"Tell me when you gone nut so I could put it in my coffee," she said in between her sucking and stroking. Ten minutes passed and she was still sucking and stroking.

"Oh shit I'm almost there, I'm 'bout to-," Patterson couldn't get the rest out as he began to shake.

She began to stroke him with her saliva on her hand and on his dick. She knew from the motions that he was 'bout to bust, so she grabbed the cup of coffee as Patterson squirted in the coffee cup.

"Thank you Mike," she said as she got up and walked out the bathroom.

"You're welcome," Patterson said as he chilled to catch his breath from what transpired.

"Hey anybody seen Patterson?" Captain Morello said as he came out his office.

Patterson heard him so he quickly forced himself to pee and get his pants together.

Captain Morello saw Officer Johnson walking away from the direction of the bathroom then that's when he peeped how Patterson came out still fixing himself up. He just shook his head as Patterson made his way into his office.

"When will you learn Patterson?" Captain Morello asked.

"What?" Patterson asked with a grin on his face.

"Wipe that stupid grin off ya face. I seen Johnson walking away from the bathroom then you come out the bathroom fixing yourself up."

"Okay you got me boss. She gave me some quick head, that's all."

"Damnit Patterson! When are you gone grow the hell up and take responsibility for you not thinking with your brain and instead always thinking with your dick? I'm gone tell you this cause I never told you before that shit is gone catch up to you."

"Man it's her fault she was talking 'bout how she-."

"I don't care what she told you. This is a professional environment, and that's why your partner left cause you was fucking his wife!" Morello shouted as he interrupted Patterson.

"Okay Captain- I'm gone try to take heed to what your telling me," Patterson said putting an end to the conversation. He was digging deep now bringing his old partner into the equation. He decided to change the tone of the conversation.

"Who's this new partner that I'm getting?" Patterson asked being inquisitive.

"Well let me tell you her name is Natasha Richmond. She moved from here from Atlanta and I'm the one that's giving her a shot. Now I would like for you to keep your dick in your pants and show her the ropes. She's gone be here by 10 a.m., its 8 now so prepare yourself you got two hours."

As Captain Morello was speaking to Patterson, Sgt. Moretti stuck his head into the office.

"Captain, me and some guys are gone step out to see if we can get some leads on that shootout that occurred last night."

"Good stay on top of that Moretti, I don't want my streets getting to out of hand," Captain Morello explained.

Before leaving, Moretti shot Detective Patterson a middle finger.

"That fucker is not doing police work Captain. I feel like that greasy haired bastard is doing some dirt on them streets I can smell it", Patterson said.

"So what you telling me? I can't trust my officers now, is that what you telling me? If that's the case, I can't trust nobody in here, not even you. Listen you keep ya mind on ya new partner and worry 'bout how you gone keep ya dick in ya pants at the job."

"Okay Captain, but don't say I didn't warn you when the shit hits the fan," Patterson stated before he left his office.

* * * * *

Erica was on her way on her way to see the most influential person in her life, her father Bishop Lamont Williams. Her father was influential because of his status on and off the pulpit. He had his own following, and was a bestselling author of a couple books he put out. He wasn't just a regular preacher or Reverend; he didn't preach the old school way. He was taught to influence the people with the word instead of telling the people what they wanted to hear. He wasn't ashamed of Erica because of her occupation; he just told her she can always do better with herself, and he wanted her to do better. Erica entered his place of worship walking straight to his office.

"Hey Daddy", Erica said as she entered his office.

"Hey Erica how's everything my child?" He asked, delighted to see her.

"I'm good daddy, just ready to make a transition."

"I like the way that sounds! Now, how's my grandson? I need to spend some quality time with him since I know his dad is not. I feel like I need to instill some good morals in my grandchild."

"Thanks, Dad. That would not be a bad idea. It would give me a quick break I need."

"Remember this-a mother's job is never done, believe it or not. When your child is old enough to think on his own, it's still your duty to teach, you see how I do you."

"I will take heed to that", Erica said.

"Now what's this transition I'm hearing about? Are you about to tell me what I'm thinking?" he asked.

"Well, what are you thinking dad?" Erica asked.

"Well I wasn't really thinking, but so just put it like this hopefully you're 'bout to tell me that you're quitting this stripping business and moving on to something more constructive instead of destructive."

"Well no, but that's how I make my living right now and I'm not ashamed of that, but I'm 'bout to get into a little acting."

Bishop Williams blew out his breath releasing frustration that was building up before he asked about what he wanted to know.

"Please tell me it's not the porn business."

"Dad. There you go. Please don't start! You always told me not to judge nobody," Erica said getting on the defensive side.

"I'm not judging you but look where you're going? I told you if you don't get out this type of business you're going to get yourself deeper in it."

"Well it's only temporary. I'm in need of some extra money since I kicked DJ's dad out."

"What happened with that?" Bishop Williams asked.

"I caught him fu—, I mean having sex with DJ's babysitter."

"Well I'm not surprised with that outcome. You found him in a place where nine times out of ten your finding someone that's gone be temporary not based on longevity, but let me ask you this Erica- why porn?"

"Dad it's only gone be temporary, but you know what I'm grown and I don't have to take this so I'm 'bout to leave."

"No don't leave yet! Help me out with this paper work and then you can leave," Bishop Williams said wanting an excuse spend more time together.

"Oh okay! Now you're gonna use me and put me to work Dad," Erica said.

"Yeah so I can show you how to do some honest work and give you some honest pay."

Erica just rolled her eyes and decided to stay and help her dad out. Plus she knew once she got busy on her new venture she probably wouldn't see him until she got time.

* * * * *

Back at the station Detective Patterson couldn't keep his mind off his new partner he was about to meet.

"I know she gone look good Captain wouldn't have said keep my dick in my pants," he thought, as he was getting anxious.

While Detective Patterson was in the act of getting himself together, she walked in. When Detective Natasha Richmond walked in any room she demanded your attention. Her walk, her clothes, her body, everything made time stop, and jaw drop. She was light brown, perky lips, chinky eyes, wore no weave, and was thick in all the right places. Her first day on the job she wanted to make the right impression so she put on an all black Donna Karen business suit, with the heels to match. Jaws dropped as she walked over to Detective Patterson to ask for Captain Morello. Mike was staring so hard his mind blanked out and he didn't hear her as she asked him to direct her to Captain Morello.

"Excuse me but where's Captain Morello's office please?" she asked again.

"Oh right this way," Patterson said as he led her to the office of the boss.

"Hello Captain Morello, I'm Natasha Richmond the new detective on the force," she said reintroducing herself to her boss.

"Yes, Detective Richmond! Glad to have you aboard, but wait, I want you to meet someone," Captain Morello said talking about Patterson.

Mike eagerly rushed in his boss's office to meet his new partner.

"Detective Richmond meet Detective Mike Patterson, Patterson meet Detective Natasha Richmond," Captain Morello said playing host.

"Nice to get acquainted with you again partner," Detective Richmond said.

"Wait do y'all already know each other?" Captain Morello asked nervously knowing how his pupil was with women.

"No, I walked up on him when I first walked in. But he was in a world of his own when I approached him," Natasha said explaining the situation.

"Oh, okay. Thank God. I was thinking the wrong thing," Captain Morello said while chuckling.

Detective Patterson looked at his boss as if to say shut the hell up.

"So I'm ready to see a couple things to learn about this beautiful city. I want to see the liberty bell, eat a cheese steak, umm what else oh yeah I want to see the steps that Rocky ran up," she stated.

"Damn! You sound like a tourist more than a detective Ms. Richmond," Mike said.

"Well if this was the other way around and you were visiting ATL, then I would show you around. Please, I've only been here for a week and I didn't get to see anything," Detective Richmond explained.

"Well let me tell you we are in West Philadelphia, the 18th district. Take a look out there, that's 55th and Pine, they don't give a damn about no liberty bell and where Rocky ran up some steps. All those people care about is how they gone eat on those streets, and they are prepared to do anything for a dollar," Patterson said.

"Well thanks for the reality check partner. Let me go get me some coffee and I will be ready to go see what's in these streets," she stated as she walked away.

"Good job breaking that down for her to get her prepared for what's out there Patterson, but remember take it light. She will learn," Captain Morello said.

Homicide City

Chapter 3

Meanwhile on the streets Sgt. Moretti was in an unmarked Crown Victoria posted on 56th and Walnut. He was pissed there was no traffic and he'd been there for almost over an hour. He decided to drive back to the station so he took 56th St. back up. As he drove up he spotted a large gathering, as the Gwap Gang were passing out flyers. Chase Money and the gang were out promoting their new party that was gone be held at the Bike Club after hour spot. As Sgt. Moretti pulled over he saw the Jamaicans that shot up the block sitting at the red light. He waited till the light turned green and threw on his siren in the dash, and pulled them over. Chase Money peeped the whole situation out as he was passing out flyers.

"Ayo! Banks, peep this shit out, look at them dumb mothafuckas still riding around wit they back window fucked up from our shootout with them."

"Oh shit they dumb as shit," Banks said while laughing.

Sgt. Moretti hopped out his vehicle and walked up on their car.

"Why the fuck y'all still riding around in this piece of shit, especially around the same area y'all shot up you dumb fucks? You see them guys that's looking over here? That's the same guys you had the shootout with. Now get rid of this piece of

45

shit," Sgt. Moretti said while pointing out the Gwap Gang.

While Moretti was telling them to leave, Chase Money was peeping the whole scene out and his bosses intuition suddenly kicked in as he put two and two together, but he didn't want to break it down to his crew while they were working he wanted them to stay focused. He decided that he was going speak to them later.

As the Jamaicans peeled off, Sgt. Moretti made his way over to the corner the Gwap Gang was on.

"You look like the smart one out of the group, let me talk to you," Moretti said talking to Chase.

"See me for what?" Chase said not feeling the situation.

"I will explain as we make it over to my car," Moretti said.

They walked over to his car and Moretti laid the business on him.

"Two things, first the shootout on 56th and Walnut I know your little gang had something to do with that. Second, that melee over Danny Wok you guys had something to do with that too. I've been watching you guys and I'm gone continue to watch you guys. I know you guys are up to no good and when I catch you guys I'm gone bury your whole gang".

"Well whoever you getting your info from is wrong we are innocent until proven guilty. We not even into the streets like that you see the shirts say GwapGang.com, we own our own website, and you can check it out for yourself. I don't know if you get down with our kind of music. It looks to me you like Frank Sinatra or something like that."

"Oh so you're a wise ass, huh? Well let me tell you, I got my eyes on you and your little gang," Moretti said getting pissed off at how Chase was coming off.

"Well I don't know why you have nothing on me and my squad, so you can keep it moving," Chase said counteracting on what Moretti said.

"Okay you want to play hard ball do you? Well we gone see what happens next," Moretti said walking away to get into his car to drive off.

"Yo Chase what that nigga wanted?" Banks asked as Chase walked back up to the block.

"Man all I'm gone say is after we hand out these flyers we gone have our sit down, but in the mean time let's focus on these flyers".

After answering Banks, Chase's phone began to ring.

"Oh shit look who it is?" Chase said holding his phone up to Banks face.

It was Stacks and Chase was excited because he knew that Stacks was calling with some good news.

"What's good, Stacks?" Chase said as he answered.

47

"Yo you know I got some good news my nigga," Stacks said.

"Yo, what's up with the block making the news I heard some crazy shit went down."

"Oh it did, but I can tell you about that later, what's this good news you got for me?"

"Oh well dig this, Chase. You know that nigga Streets the boy that's behind the In Da Streets DVD? He wants to put us on his Hottest In Da Streets DVD."

"Oh shit that's what's up, the whole city look at that DVD," Chase said getting excited about the news knowing it meant more exposure for the crew.

"I know. That's why I'm calling you Chase tell everybody cause he want to record us ASAP."

"Cool I will make sure I holla at everybody, when the next time you coming out West?"

"When we film the DVD."

"Alright Stacks. We grinding passing out these flyers for the upcoming show so I will holla at you later my nigga."

* * * * *

Detective Richmond was ready to get a glimpse of the streets after she drunk her coffee and got her desk together. As she and Detective Patterson walked out to his car, Moretti was pulling up. Moretti parked behind the precinct to avoid running into Patterson.

"You see him right there pulling up, that's Frank Moretti, you see how's he's avoiding me? He dirty and I know it and I'm gone prove it to Captain Morello."

"Well how do you know he's dirty?" Richmond asked.

"For one his last name is Moretti and I think that he is connected with the Moretti family. All I got to do is prove it and get his mozzarella eating ass out of here."

"Well you know you have to present evidence to prove that right you just can't go off the bad hunch you have," Richmond explained.

"Oh believe me, when I say that I am," Patterson said, "Okay now partner since I have your attention, I'm hungry and I'm taking you to my favorite spot on 52nd St. to get breakfast, just keep your eyes open and enjoy the ride."

They hopped in his Luzerne and the journey began. "On ya right hand side that's Malcolm X park", Patterson said while driving up more. "Now on ya left right here is the church that belongs to Bishop Lamont Williams. I never been inside but I hear he is the man to talk to when you need some type of direction."

As they drove past, Erica was coming out of the church.

"Damn and speaking of helping people that would be the perfect person to lead," Patterson said commenting on Erica as he rolled down his window.

"Hey baby you looking good today, did you enjoy the good word for the day?" Patterson asked flirting with her.

Erica just rolled her eyes and ignored Patterson and kept it moving since she was hungry after helping her father out with his paperwork.

"So I see you're a ladies' man," Detective Richmond said commenting on her partners actions she just witnessed.

"I do alright with the ladies," Patterson said trying not to brag.

He ended up driving across Chestnut and Market to get to his destination which was named Yummy's. As he was driving he noticed that a money green Escalade with tinted windows was following him. The Escalade parked a block down from where he parked but he made sure he was gone keep an eye out on whoever was following him.

"Look partner, I don't know if you noticed but that Escalade has been on my ass ever since I was driving here so could you keep an eye out on it."

"I'm going in with you so how is that going to be possible?" Richmond asked.

"Okay well c'mon then," Patterson directed as they hopped out to order their food.

As they walked in Patterson was greeted as the man of the day as always.

"Hey look who it is! It's Mr. Patterson," the owner Yummy said, "Now who do you have with you? She's beautiful! Is this your new girlfriend, Mike?"

"Naw, naw this is my new partner Yummy," Mike answered.

"Okay now what you ordering the usual, home fries, eggs, and turkey bacon?"

"You know what I was thinking that I should switch to grits today," Patterson answered while rubbing his stomach.

"Okay now that we got you out of the way. What about your partner?"

"Uh, I want 2 pancakes, turkey bacon, and eggs scrambled with cheese please," Detective Richmond said.

"Okay that's gone be 15-20 minutes," Yummy said after taking their orders.

"Good gives me time to go spark a Newport," Patterson said.

"I'm right behind you partner," Natasha said.

As they walked out, two men were approaching them. Patterson was tapping his pockets for his lighter.

"Damn. Left my lighter in the car," he said out loud.

"Need a light, my man?" one of the men asked as they stopped in front them.

"Thanks man," Patterson said while sparking his Newport and not even knowing the men.

"Can I help you guys with something?" Patterson asked not understanding why they were just standing there and was staring.

"Yes you can help me out. I want to know why you fucking my wife?" one of the guys asked.

"Who's your wife? Cause let me tell you I fuck plenty of bitches so it's hard for me to remember," Patterson said bragging on his dick.

"Aneesa," the man answered.

"Oh, Aneesa! I didn't know she was married man she didn't tell me, so my bad if that's your wife."

"Well yeah I'm her husband and I'm here to tell you to stay the fuck away from my wife. I don't care if you're a cop I will bury you 6ft!"

"Man, go 'head wit' all the drama, before I lock ya dumb ass up for threatening a detective."

"Man fuck you!" the guy shouted as his homie tried to calm him down.

Patterson was calm as he took a puff of his Newport then blew the smoke in the guys face. As he was done taking his puff he flicked his Newport on the ground and stared at the man. Aneesa's husband then pulled out a knife and threatened Patterson.

"If I ever here that you touched my wife again, or you was even near her I swear I'm gone cut ya"....POW! A gunshot rang out.

He'd just been shot in the leg,

Detective Richmond came to the aid of her partner and put a hot one in the man's leg. Patterson couldn't believe how fast the situation happened; he was a little stunned.

"Damn, Richmond! You had to shoot him though, man. I had the situation covered."

"I felt like you was reacting too slowly, so I had to shoot him."

"Look sharp shooter! Take this twenty and get our food, and please get me a water while I take care of this situation. Damn. This is gone be some long paperwork," Patterson said as he gathered the man up to cuff him.

The man was still in pain from the leg shot as he began to yell out obscenities.

"That bitch shot me! She didn't have to shoot me!" he yelled out.

"Well you shouldn't have brought a knife to a gun fight pussy", Detective Richmond said as she walked out of Yummy's with their platters.

* * * * *

Erica was starving her ass off as she pulled up on 56th and Spruce at Hyon's Seafood to grab her a platter. As she pulled up at Hyon's she noticed the Gwap Gang outside promoting their show/party.

"Hey Chase, what's up?" Erica yelled out as she went into Hyon's.

"Aye y'all, I be right back let me holla at her real quick," Chase said to his squad.

Erica was ordering her scallops, chicken wings, and fries platter as Chase walked up on her to holla at her bout the show he wanted to get established at the club she dances at.

53

"Yo Erica we gone be at the Bike club on 63rd and Market Fri. You should swing through."

"Cool Chase! If I have time I will definitely swing through."

"What's up wit' ya boss? Did you holla at him yet?"

"You know what? I didn't. I'm sorry, but when were you trying to do something? I can call him right now while I'm waiting on my food?"

"You know what Erica now that you said something, I know its last minute but ask him for this Saturday."

"Alright cool," Erica said as she pulled out her cell and dialed Benji's number.

"Benji, what's up boss man? I got this business man beside me that's trying to rent out your club to do a video/performance this Saturday."

"Alright cool tell him as long as my club don't get shot up it's a go. I don't care you know I'm all about them benjis," Benji said on the other end of her phone.

"Cool, but how much it's gone cost him to do it Benji?" Erica asked.

"Tell the man 2 stacks for the night. That's all since he ya peoples."

"Cool Benji, thank you for the favor and I'm gone give him the rundown," Erica said hanging up with Benji.

"Yo that means it's gone be a crazy weekend," Chase said getting excited 'bout how everything was working out for him, "Yo you still doing the video right?" Chase asked Erica.

"Hell yeah. Now how much I'm getting paid for doing the video?" Erica asked.

"Since you looked out for me I will give you a stack. Now do you got some connects with some of your girlfriends to dance with you in the video?"

"Now I'm gone need more money if you want me putting in that type of work organizing for you."

"Okay cool. Five stacks and that's my final offer," Chase demanded.

"You got it Chase," Erica agreed.

"I'm gone have the flyers for that show done tomorrow, and I'm gone catch up to you," Chase said as they exchanged cell phones numbers before he left out to get back to promoting with his squad.

"Wow! I'm becoming a business woman," Erica said to herself as she grabbed her food and left Hyon's.

Homicide City

Chapter 4

Erica made it to her house, and decided to call the Triple X Production producer.

"Triple X productions. This is Candice speaking. How may I help you?" the receptionist said as she answered.

"Yes Candice I'm looking for Brian "Action" Jackson."

"Yes hold on while I transfer you to his office."

"Hello. Brian "Action" Jackson, producer extraordinaire. How can I assist you?" the man answered.

"Yes Brian. My name is Erica."

"Yes, I have been waiting for your call. Now, are you ready Erica?"

"Well, tell me what I need to be ready for."

"Are you ready to make money?"

"Yes I'm ready to make money. I was born to make money."

"Cool. I'm looking for a lead role in my new movie Head Doctors, so let me ask you are you gone be busy later because you can audition tonight, then if you get the part we could start filming soon."

"Okay I can be there by five. Is that cool with you, Brian?"

"Yes that's perfect", Brian answered, "Oh and please Erica wear something nice to impress me, I love to be impressed."

"Okay I will impress you then, but let me go. I got to prepare for the audition," Erica said before they hung up.

"Damn, I'm glad I didn't smoke that other dub of Kush," she said to herself as she grabbed a Dutch and proceeded to cracking it to roll up.

After perfectly rolling up her Kush, she went to work on her scallop, chicken wing, and French fry platter. If she was eating next to someone they would've been so annoyed from the smacking she was doing. She didn't even cut on the T.V. She was so focused on eating the platter. It only took her ten minutes to demolish it.

"I'm glad I work out. I would be so fat," Erica said out loud to herself while grabbing a lighter to blaze her Dutch up.

While in-between puffs she was contemplating on how she was going to impress this producer.

That nigga think he fooling somebody. He probably want some quick pussy then I would get the part. He bet not try and scam a bitch either cause I will definitely cut his dick off in the process she thought to herself.

* * * * *

Sgt. Moretti told Captain Morello he was taking his lunch, but the truth was he was on his way to a meeting with his real boss Tony Moretti

"Just get your ass here we are waiting for you," Tony said through the receiver without even saying hello then hanging up. He was running late,

Sgt. Moretti couldn't even get in a word. Tony hung up on him so fast.

"Fuck it. Let me get there before he has a heart attack," Moretti said to himself.

As he walked into the café, he went straight over to Tony Moretti and gave him a kiss on the cheek and then greeted everyone else with handshakes.

"Now that Frank is here we can start this meeting," Tony said as Sgt. Moretti sat down.

Sgt. Moretti wasn't even related to Tony Moretti, but since he was an enforcer for him and opened up lanes for him to operate, Tony embraced him and gave him the last name. This pertained to 25% of other people that was in the room too, the other 75% were full-blooded Moretti's.

"Now the reason for this meeting is this Kush product we are about to invest in. Frank over here is talking to the Jamaicans since they grow it, and they are letting us put it out in the street. So with that being said who's ready to expand and put their money in the pot so we can get everything in motion? Frank is going to enforce everything now all we need is the financial backing of the rest of the family".

After Tony was done speaking his three younger brothers took off their pinky rings and put them in the middle of the table to signify that they were in. That's all Tony needed to see as he took off his and the deal was closed.

"Now it's all about expansion with product like this, so three parts of the city is good right now to start off," Tony said as he was going down the line of parts of the city he was focused on.

"Frank, how's things on the west side?" Tony asked.

"Umm... I'm still ironing out things but everything should be moving in a minute," he answered.

"Well get them straight. I don't need any fuck ups on this deal. It's too sweet, with this money we bout to get our hands on we could open up another club or something."

"Now Paul you gone get South Philly in order, Michael you gone get the Northeast area, last but not least Don you gone expand in North Philly. Now before I end this meeting does anybody object to what transpired in the meeting?"

Nobody said anything. Tony and his brothers picked up their pinky rings and it was official. Everybody got up to as Tony pulled Sgt. Moretti to the side to talk to him about how he was handling business.

"Listen King told me the stunt you pulled over there, I don't like how you enforced that move," Tony said speaking with sincerity.

"But Tony," before Frank could finish his reply his face was greeted with a slap.

"Listen to me. How can you get someone to move with you after trying to kill them? It doesn't make sense. Frank, I pulled you into the family to make the right decisions and that wasn't what I wanted to happen. Now you have to clean that up, and I expect you to do so."

"Okay Tony I will clean it up," Sgt. Moretti said as he rubbed the side of his face where it still burned from the slap.

* * * * *

Back at the station Captain Morello was tearing Detective Patterson and Richmond new assholes from the incident on 52nd St.

"Richmond what the hell possessed you to just shoot the man? I mean tell me, cause I know y'all could've handled the situation much more better than y'all did," he scolded.

"Okay Captain, once again, the way I reacted I felt was the best way. The man pulled out a knife on my partner. Then when that happened I felt like the both of us were in harm's way so I gave him a leg shot to deescalate the situation."

"Now onto you Patterson, why did the guy approach you the way he did?" Morello asked, knowing his detective was always in some shit.

"Okay sir the guy knew I was fucking his wife so he tried to poke me up."

"See I told you, didn't I tell you ya dick would get you in trouble? I hope you learned ya lesson with this situation."

"Well what's the charges you have on this guy?" Captain Morello asked.

Detective Richmond decided to answer his question.

"Threatening an officer of the law, brandishing a illegal weapon, and attempted assault with a deadly weapon," Richmond answered thoroughly.

"Now after the situation did y'all run his name to see if had any priors or warrants?" Captain Morello asked trying to cover all angles.

"Yes we did, but he didn't have any of the above," Patterson answered.

"So just to let y'all two know since he's not a violent offender this is not gone stick but we will see. These are his first charges so I don't think he's gone receive any time for this, but this does add a court date to y'all personal time."

"Well okay now can we get back to the paperwork," Detective Patterson said sounding like he was getting pissed that he even had to do paperwork.

"Well you wouldn't need to do paperwork if ya dick wasn't making the rules," Captain Morello said, "But since you're in a rush to get that done I need that before y'all two leave for the day."

They both left the office and got back to filling out the paperwork at their desks.

"Thanks partner! First day on the job and I got to give a man a leg shot!" Detective Richmond exclaimed.

"Well that part of the job comes with the territory, but let me just tell you I loved the one liner you gave him, and may I quote you, 'you shouldn't have brought a knife to a gun fight, pussy'," Patterson said trying to sound just like his partner as they both laughed.

"I see this is just the beginning of a crazy partnership," Detective Richmond said.

"Yeah buckle ya seat belt," Patterson said as they got back to writing out their paperwork.

* * * * *

As Erica entered the lobby of the building of where Triple X Productions resided, she caught the eye of the grey-haired guard from what she had on for the audition. She had on an all black skirt that had straps that made an X like shape that covered her breasts that hugged her body like a bear hug. To top it off three inch heels that when she walked her ass shook like Jell-O.

"Yes sir. I'm here to go to an audition for Triple X Productions," Erica said as she walked up.

"Y-y-y-yes, he's on the seventh floor," the old man stuttered from the sight of Erica and what she had on.

"Oooh, my lucky number," Erica said.

As Erica went to the elevator she could feel the old man's eyes beaming on her ass.

"Take a picture. It'll last longer," Erica let out knowing the man was staring at her ass as she walked to the elevator.

But it was too late. The guard already had pulled out his cell phone to take a picture and make a video of her walking to the elevator. Erica made it to the seventh floor, then stepped off the elevator and walked into the offices of Triple X Productions.

As she walked in, she went straight for the receptionist desk where Candice was sitting.

"Yes may I help you?" Candice asked politely as Erica walked up.

"Yes, I'm here for the audition with Brian Jackson," Erica answered.

"Oh you must be Erica. Hold on. I can get him on the line, but let me tell you girl you are wearing that dress."

"Thanks," Erica said.

"Yes Candice," Brian said on the speaker.

"Mr. Jackson you have Erica here for her audition."

"Okay, I'll be right out in a minute."

"So Candice, how many girls make it in this business?" Erica asked.

"It's about the money, but really you have to stay strong, cause if you dive straight in the sharks will eat you alive. But you control everything you have to stay on top of your game and go for the lead part instead of just being a feature cause being lead is where the money is at."

"Thanks for the insight, now have you ever starred in a porno?"

"Yes, that's how I got this job. This is my second job. I'm learning how to become a receptionist so I can land me an office job, and I do the porno on the side. As you can see I'm about my paper, girl."

"Yeah I can see that. A blind man would be able to see that," Erica stated.

As they were talking, Brian Jackson was walking down the hallway coming to greet Erica for the first time. As he walked up his eyes lit up from how she looked.

"Goddamn," he thought he said to himself but spoke aloud.

"Thank you, Mr. Jackson. Now you said impress you, so hopefully that's what I did."

"Yes. You did," Brian responded.

"Is everything cool out here Candice?" Brian asked.

"Yes everything is good. I got my jet magazines and I'm on the Internet shopping for new shoes. My time is definitely moving."

"Well alright that's what I like to hear. Now Erica, you can follow me to my office."

They walked to his office and he closed the door behind them after they entered. As he sat down he got straight into business.

"Now let me tell you this is the process for every movie I do. I give everybody a chance to get their spots, I have four features and one person that gets the lead part. I already have four girls for the feature slots, now all I need is to find the one for the lead part to be on the cover and you would end the movie. What's that saying people say save the best for last that's what I do. Also the movie is strictly an oral movie so if you object do so now."

"Keep going I don't object," Erica said.

"Okay, the movie is going to be called Head Doctors, and a little dialogue will be written out for you to say, but when all that is done you have to give the patient head. Now let me ask you this since you didn't object, are you skilled in the oral department?"

"Yes I'm very skilled in that department Mr. Jackson," she answered.

"So when are you gone be ready to audition?" Brian asked.

"You mean right here, right now audition?" Erica asked.

"Yes, this is your test. If you pass you get the lead role and 5,000 dollars," Brian said as he stood up and walked over to her.

"Okay", she answered as she unzipped his pants. Her eyes lit up as she pulled out his dick.

"You ain't even hard yet and it's this big? Damn, I can only imagine how big it's gone get!" she exclaimed as she stared at the four inches. She inserted the whole thing in her mouth and started licking and sucking at the same time.

"You must really want this part," Brian said in amazement after seeing her take his whole dick to her throat, "Now keep impressing me and I will give you the part and throw in a extra grand if you do that while I'm all the way hard."

Erica quickly got him hard by sucking and gliding her tongue on the tip of his dick. As he grew in inches she began to doubt that she was going to be able to take all what she saw to the back of her throat.

"So how big is it, Mr. Jackson?" Erica said as she began to jerk him off.

"You don't need to know that now. Matter of fact, I will let you know after you accomplish it."

Erica took a deep breath, then opened her mouth and let his dick slide all the way back to her throat. She gagged as it hit the back of her throat.

Brian knew he had her right where he needed her to be and he could smell how vulnerable she was after the fact that he included the five grand and a little extra. So he decided to take it to another level.

"You know what Erica? I'm not that convinced with just you taking my dick to the back of your throat, now with knowing you come from a stripper background and judging by the way that body looks, I want to see the whole package."

He was right. Erica was in a vulnerable state of mind where she couldn't say no. Her mind was thinking about that five grand she was offered, so she replied like any desperate person would.

"Okay what else would you like to see?"

"Let me see you bend over and touch your toes," Brian said in a freaky manner.

"Wow this is too easy," Erica thought to herself as she stood up and bent over for Brian. It was easy for her to do since she already did that at the club. Brian stared in amazement at the sight for about a good ten seconds, then proceeded to grab a condom from out his draw and slid it on his ten inches. As he slid in her wet walls Erica let out a moan and slither on her tongue to signify how good it felt. Brian went to work like a dog in heat, stroking in and out to tame his new protégé. Every stroke came with a moan and the moans got even louder for Erica as she came. After giving her the business standing up, Brian decided to switch it up. He then grabbed her and put her on the leather couch that was in his office and told her to make the letter Y with her legs. After she followed the orders, he slid right back in noticing she was even wetter than before.

"Damn. How many times you cum Erica?" Brian asked through heavy breathing.

"Ooh twice baby, twice," Erica repeated through moans and heavy breathing.

This turned Brian on as he sped up his strokes and went deeper in her pussy. He was a seasoned vet on how he controlled his climaxes and knew that he was 'bout to cum so he quickly took off the condom and started to stroke his self. Before he could finish Erica took control.

"Let me take care of that for you," said as she stroked and sucked until he came in her mouth.

"Wow, look at that! You passed the test and you get an extra grand on top of that five I gave you."

"Now you got to tell me how long it is?" Erica said.

"Ten inches," Brian answered as he gave her the check she was promised.

"Thank you," Erica said as she took the check.

"Now Erica. I will call you soon when it's time to start filming."

"Okay Mr. Jackson I'll be waiting for your call," Erica said as she walked out.

"So did you get the part?" Candice asked as Erica walked up from the office.

Erica walked over to the desk excited and showed her the check.

"Yes I did and let me tell you my throat still feel funny from taking all his dick to my throat."

"Well let me tell you that's only the beginning Erica," Candice said.

"Thank you Candice, I will holla at you later girl. I'm going to deposit this check."

* * * * *

Meanwhile, across town, The Gwap Gang was having a meeting on what took place while they were passing out their flyers. As usual, Chase Money, being the boss, he had the platform to speak first.

"Listen up y'all. We got a problem on our hands. I wanted to speak on it while we were passing out the flyers but I wanted us to stay focused, but this is what's going down we setting up shop on another block and right now I'm thinking the best move is 54th St."

Before he could finish, everybody showed how disgruntled they were to the change that was taking place.

"I know this is very short notice but we have to move this way according to what took place."

"So what took place to where we have to move like we scared?" Banks said being the first to speak up.

"It's not about being scared Banks. This is chess not checkers," Chase said, "Now let me further enlighten you about my convo with the cop. He told me that he knows that 56th and Walnut is ours so he must have been the culprit of putting together that hit to move us out. Also he even bought up the Danny Wok situation. Now fuck the Danny Wok scuffle that shit is a mole as far as I'm concerned, and I'm not in the business of making moles into mountains. I'm here discussing paper and what's the best move we need to make to continue getting it like we do without the heat."

"Okay makes sense now Chase," Banks said.

"Now does anybody disagree on the move we need to make, if so speak up now."

Nobody disagreed with Chase's request but people still had things to get off their chest about how they should move.

"Okay well what's up with this cop character? Do we need to keep an eye on him?" Scrilla asked.

"Man fuck him, as long we are out of sight we don't need to be worried about him," Chase answered, "All we need to be concerned about is getting our paper and making the right moves".

"Cool," Scrilla said.

"Yeah. That's all man. We already focused. Let's not fall off cause some little cop is trying to bring us down," Banks added, latching on to the leadership that Chase always brought to the table.

"Now that we got the bad news out of the way, let's move onto some good news. I received a call from Stacks today saying the boy Streets want us to be on his upcoming DVD Hottest In the Streets."

"For real Chase? Yo ,the streets be buzzing about the boy DVDs. Everybody and the momma be buying the In Da Streets DVD. If we get on that DVD, we will have the whole city in a frenzy," Scrilla said.

"Yeah I know. That would definitely be a good look for us we could promote the website and show niggas why we the hottest niggas," Chase said.

"Yeah it's time for us to let all them niggas know who the hottest," Banks said confidently.

"I know I'm ready. I've been writing some hot shit," Scrilla said.

"Yeah me too," Paperboi said.

"That's what's up and y'all better let them niggas have it, I want the whole city to know that Gwap Gang got next," Chase said.

* * * * *

Rap DVDs are one of the quickest ways to get hot in the streets if you want to make it in the rap world. The Gwap Gang knew this so that's why they saw the opportunity to be on The Hottest In the Streets DVD as a golden one. Streets met up with them on 56th and Walnut as he prepared them to how the interview was gone go.

"So basically I want get y'all set up with just introducing yourselves to the streets plus tell them what's going on in y'all world," Streets said setting while setting up his camera.

"Cool," Chase Money said.

The Gwap Gang made sure they were prepared for the DVD. They all had on their fresh GwapGang.com T-shirts, respectively. Chase made sure no one wore their jewelry to make it look like they were still on the grind. Even though they were, he didn't want to bring any unwanted attention to their other grind in the streets since the cops be watching the DVDs.

"You're live right now with Streets and I have in front of me one of the hottest groups in Philly on the come up, The Gwap Gang. Aye fellas, could we do a roll call for the streets?"

"Definitely, I'm the ultimate hustler always on the paper chase Chase Money."

"And I'm his right hand the Capo out of the crew, Banks."

"They call me Paperboi cause I know how to get that paper boy."

"Yeah, it's ya boy Scrilla the nicest young boy in the city repping that Gwap Gang."

"And it's the man with the platinum hands Stacks the man behind the hits."

"Now that the streets are familiar let them know what's going on with the Gwap Gang."

"Aww man it's a lot going on with us just take a look at the shirts and read GwapGang.com that explains it all," Chase Money said answering the first question.

"Any mix tapes or albums the streets should know about?"

"Oh yeah they can check us out on that Gwap Ova Everything E.P we released if they didn't already cop that," Banks said stepping in front of the camera.

"Yeah tell a friend and go tell a friend to download the hottest E.P in the streets, they can check me out I did all the production," Stacks said getting his shine on in the camera.

"So what's the numbers on the project so far?"

"5,000 downloads and 1,000 ring tones and we ain't stunting on y'all we just stating facts," Chase Money said stepping into boss mode continuing on.

"We did all this from grinding in the streets. We not looking for a deal. We independent. All that money comes straight back to the US. We promote our own shows we do it straight from the muscle. Anybody wants to sign us gone have to cut us a seven-figure check. You know what I mean?"

"Oh yeah I feel you that's huge numbers independently now let's get to the rapping, I think the streets wanna hear some of that platinum independence y'all speaking on."

"Okay well that's not a problem. Just like my boy stated he the hottest young boy in the streets get 'em Scrilla."

Scrilla stepped up in the camera and set it off representing for his whole crew.

"Whoever say they fucking wit Gwap Gang I tell ''em nigga, please,

We hustle hard touch more cream then Philadelphia cheese,

West Philly born, West Philly raised,

My eyes stay red we smoke on the best haze,

And when it comes to ya chicks you better pull out ya handcuffs,

Cause I'm a pimp I get all in her head my mans call me dandruff,

And ever since sixteen I was spitting the hottest sixteen,

Cause I all I need is the paper like a fax machine,

Next year Gwap Gang we in the hottest cars getting all the bitches,

And whoever hate y'all niggas can sleep with the fishes,

So whoever wants war we got bullets for each and all of y'all,

I can put three in ya head, have you looking like a bowling ball.

The whole Gwap Gang went crazy when they heard the new rhymes come from one of the youngest out of the crew.

"Yeah I hope y'all niggas was paying attention, that's what we call hot right there. I don't know what y'all call hot but we the hottest. What's this DVD called the hottest in the streets, that's what I call the hottest in the streets?" Chase Money said after his young soldier just put in work on the camera.

"I know it's like five of y'all so who's up next," Streets said.

"I'm up next, I got something for the streets," Banks said.

"Get 'em Banks!" Chase Money, Scrilla, and Paperboi chanted from the side before Banks started his lyrical arsenal.

"They call me the O.G out the crew that keeps smuts on my penis,

Cause I ball hard carry my hammer like Gilbert arenas,

Its ya boy banks I keep my pockets fat like Phillips,

And if I was broke like Chauncey I would make you give ya bills up

But we balling ova here swish from the bass line,

Hate and you can catch hollows from what I carry on my waistline,

We don't waste time G.O.E is the gang motto,

Hammers can leave you headless like Sleep Hollow,
But this ain't no fairytale this is real life,
Gwap Gang we switch whips like transvestites,
Cause all we do is grind get it from the curb,
Last haters I gave 'em 3 from the hammer like Larry Bird.

"Yo you live with ya boy Streets and that shit was hot, we don't need to hear no more I'm convinced that the Gwap Gang y'all the Hottest In Da Streets," Streets said as he was filming.

"See that's why we able to move those units off our website, what y'all niggas thought we were lying Gwap Gang we the hottest in the streets. You see the T-shirt log on GwapGang.com download the E.P or cop the ring tone," Chase Money added before Streets was done recording.

"Yo I like y'all young niggas, I tell you what hit me up whenever y'all got some shows so I can get more footage of y'all," Streets said jumping on the Gwap Gang bandwagon.

"That's cool we got a big one coming up soon," Chase Money said pulling out his cell phone taking his number.

The whole Gwap Gang gave Streets a handshake before he left, then he jumped in his burgundy Grand Marquis and pulled off from their block. The Gwap Gang was left feeling like they ruled the world at the moment. But with all the love

they knew they were gone receive from the footage
the hate was soon to follow.

Homicide City

Chapter 5

Judge McClain slammed his gavel at the night court hearing to see if Aneesa's husband would get bail. The only reason why he got bail was because he wasn't a violent offender. These were his first charges plus the judge felt his pain.

"I'm hungry," Detective Richmond said as they left the hearing.

"Well I got a spot we could hit it's a nice soul food spot on 60th and Haverford," Detective Patterson said.

"Good. Let's go," Natasha agreed.

As they were driving Natasha sparked conversation.

"Mike do you mind if I tell you something?"

"Naw I don't mind at all. Let's shoot the breeze."

"You don't remind me of a cop, you remind me of a model."

"Everybody says that, but this is where I'm at with my life. Eventually I want to invest in something to benefit me but I'm helping the community right now."

"Well you know you helping the people you forget to help yourself?"

"Yeah I know partner, it's like a double-edged sword," Detective Patterson said as they pulled up to GiGi's Restaurant.

As they hopped out the car Detective Richmond began to look around.

"Why you looking around like that?" Patterson asked.

"I'm making sure none of your little girlfriends husbands don't run up on us," Detective Richmond said, making herself laugh.

"Oh I see you got jokes right now. It's cool. I know I got dick issues. Quick draw McGraw."

Detective Patterson's comment made them both crack up at each other's jokes while entering the restaurant. Detective Patterson ordered fish, yams, and macaroni and cheese, while Detective Richmond ordered stewed chicken, rice and beans, and string beans. As they were enjoying their meals Detective Patterson decided to finally grill his partner.

"So how old are you?" he asked respectively.

"I'm 30 years old," she answered.

"Wow. You told me without having a problem with me asking. You're the first woman I met to ever do that."

"Well I'm past all that not revealing age bull crap women be throwing out there. I say that any woman that doesn't like to reveal their age has an insecure problem about their age and I'm not insecure about my age. I look and feel 21 so I have no problems."

"Well okay you didn't have to go that deep into it, but where have you been staying for the last month? You been in the city and what made you come to Philly?"

"Damn, you digging deep, ain't you?" Detective Richmond said sounding like she was getting defensive.

"Well I'm trying to get to know my partner," Detective Patterson answered.

"I'm just joking with you. My mom lives up here and she a little sick right now and my cousin goes to U of Penn, and oh we have a condo together."

"Okay now what's up with your dad?"

"Well my dad he's down ATL getting his hustle on with Internet businesses and Real Estate."

"Now back to ya mom. What's up with this sickness you told me about?"

"Well supposedly they found a little lump in one of her breasts that has been making her weak, so they have to do surgery and I'm here to give her support."

"Sorry to hear that I hope she gets better."

"No don't say you hope, she is, and I don't think I can't take losing her right now."

Natasha decided to switch up the tone of the conversation since she was getting a little emotional.

"Now what's up with you Mr. can't keep his dick in his pants?"

Her statement caused laughter to come between them.

"Well what do you want to know?" Patterson asked.

"Well I know you have a penis problem, but do you have kids?"

"Yes, I have one son and he's five."

"Well I know you have baby mama drama right, plus let me guess she's not with you cause you couldn't keep ya dick together, and to top it off you get it from ya dad?"

"How do you know?" Patterson asked being inquisitive.

"Well people don't understand the science of life, all that situation is a generational curse, that's all."

"Yeah I know all about those," Patterson said agreeing with his partner, "But I keeps it moving cause I already know the apple doesn't fall far from the tree."

"Yeah but enough of all that where do you live at?" Detective Richmond asked changing the tone of the conversation again.

"I'm on City Ave, got a condo you know I'm enjoying life right now."

"That's good. Now what's up with your parents?"

"Well, you know, my parent's situation is identical to yours. They not together, but they both live in Philly."

"Cool. Now that we are done eating, let's go get something to drink."

"I know the perfect place to go," Patterson said as they got up paid their bill and left.

* * * * *

Sgt. Moretti knew he needed two good men on his side if he wanted to pull off the plans he put together. So he handpicked two men that he knew were reliable and loyal within the Moretti family that wanted to rise in the ranks and show that had what it takes to pull off anything they wanted. He handpicked Joey "Five Fingers" and Johnny "Capers" Moretti. He met up with them outside a strip club Tony Moretti owned on Passyunk Ave.

"So what's the job, Frankie?" Johnny asked as they both hopped in Frank's car.

"Yeah so I know y'all heard that we got a connect on this new Kush product."

"Yeah I heard about that," Joey said getting in on the convo.

"It's a Jamaican named King in West Philly, he owns a bar called Studio 7. He grows the product himself and needed people to move it now that's where Tony and the family come in at. Now I'm taking you guys on a little home invasion party and we gone take some of the product to come up more along with what we investing in."

"Wow! Good plan, Frankie! Did Tony put you up to this?" Johnny asked.

"What you think? I can't come up with a good plan? Listen to me and listen good. Tony would never have made me enforcer if I couldn't make decisions like this for the family. He knows nothing about these plans but believe me these moves are for the family and the family only."

Even though Sgt. Moretti was lying, he knew he had to make it sound good to them, but deep down he was making this move entirely for himself. He just knew once it went down he had to pass off a couple of dollars to the both of them to keep them quiet.

"Now after this job, don't go around bragging to him like y'all some big shots. I will let him know who put in this work with me," Sgt. Moretti said gassing their heads up.

"Okay. We cool with that," the both of them agreed in unison.

Sgt. Moretti drove around Cobbs Creek until he came around 58th St. and made a left to drive up to Baltimore Ave. As he approached Baltimore he drove straight as he crossed the light and drove up 58th until he came up on Spruce St. then made a left on Spruce. He then drove up to 60th and Spruce and pulled over and parked in the cut to peep the scene out.

"Look here's the club right here. Now all we have to do is wait here until a black Suburban pulls up and takes us to the jackpot," Sgt. Moretti said explaining the situation.

They waited for almost a half hour and that's when the black Suburban pulled up. The Suburban dropped off King and a couple of his men as they walked into Studio 7, and the Suburban waited just sat in front of the club for a couple of minutes, until they got the word that it was cool to leave. After a couple of minutes passed by, the Suburban took off straight up 60th St. By this time Sgt. Moretti was tailing its every move. As they came up on Walnut, the truck made a left onto the one way and drove up until it came up on 61st and Walnut and made another left and drove straight up until they came up on 61st and Pine then pulled over.

"This is a perfect spot for an invasion. Nobody will know as long as it's no casualties. I got clean revolvers just in case they are some the bullets will walk with us. Now are the both of y'all ready?"

"Yeah," both of them said as they put on their ski masks and hopped out to take care of their business.

* * * * *

Detective Richmond and Patterson were at Scooter's enjoying music and drinks with all the other cops on that side of town.

"So how many of these cops' wives you fuck Patterson?" Natasha asked.

"Let's see…about half," Patterson answered as they burst out laughing at his reply. "I mean look at this face. How can any bitch resist this face? Plus, I'm fresh every day. I make sure of that, so basically they can't help themselves."

"Well let me tell you and this ain't no come on or anything but I can see why," Richmond said talking about her partner's swagger.

They were both buzzing from taking two shots of Patron and downing two Coronas when Detective Patterson's phone went off. He stepped into the bathroom to take the call as he saw it was Captain Morello.

"What's up boss man? What can I do for you at the moment?"

"Mike go over to 61st and Pine now a couple of bodies dropped and I need you to get over there ASAP."

"Cool Captain. I'll be there in 15 minutes."

Patterson quickly hung up his phone, took a piss, and left the bathroom.

"Let's go partner. We got some action."

Chapter 6

Detective Patterson and Richmond pulled up on 61st and Pine incognito.

"Wow. This looks bad", Detective Richmond said as they parked.

"Hey guys, what's up?" Officer Freeman asked. "I was the first on the scene, and then came Moretti its crazy in there. It looks like a home invasion gone bad on a couple of drug dealers."

"Cool," Patterson said as everyone walked over to the house.

They could see a couple of neighborhood folks being nosy wanting to know what happened, also Action News and NBC News were pulling up on the scene at the same time.

Right when Detective Patterson and Richmond made it inside, they smelled the aroma of Kush.

"Damn! You smell that?" Richmond asked her partner.

"Hell yeah and I wish I had some to smoke," Patterson commented.

They walked in the first room where the first two bodies were laid out. Patterson removed the white sheets and the first thing he noticed was they both had dreads. Two more bodies were lying at the top of the steps, and they too had dreads.

"Okay Richmond take notes that all victims have dreads and headshot wounds. No body shots. Next, we got to get the identities of the victims. Listen before y'all take these bodies out get their fingerprints," Patterson said making his way through the crime scene. "Alright now since we got the bodies taken care of let's see what we can find in the rooms,"

As they walked down the hallway, they entered the master bedroom and saw that the wall was torn.

"Wow must be some potent shit if it's not in here and we can still smell it," Richmond said commenting on the high grade Kush that was in the room before the robbery.

"Yeah it must be, I wish whoever took it would've dropped a dime or something before they left," Patterson said, " But let me ask you partner show me where ya head is at on this so-called invasion."

"Well first of all, I didn't see any shell casings so that means the shooters had revolvers. I know there was multiple shooters because if it was only one then it would be impossible to walk out of here with four people and not get hit, and there would been a different blood on the scene. I see a robbery turned bad but they were in and out, so we might be dealing with some cowboys here and shall I add their good they know what they came for and they got it."

Patterson was blown away by her observation and how she broke down the scenario.

"Good work, Richmond! All we got to see who these bodies point to and build our case from there," Patterson added, "All I got to say is Welcome to Homicide City, Richmond."

One of King's men was on the scene peeping from an alley on what was going on. He knew from the location that it was one of King's houses so he decided to make that call to King.

"King one of your houses being looked at by the cops, ya hear me?"

"Get out of the area I don't want nobody to see you. I will find out what's going on," he replied, quickly hanging up the phone.

Right after King hung up with him, he dialed Sgt. Moretti's number.

"Moretti what happened ova dere at my house and why are the cops there?"

"Okay look King, we got some renegades on the loose, they went in took ya pounds and killed four of your workers."

"They killed me men and stole me product? Find out who in the hell would steal from me right now or I will cause a blood bath, ya hear me now?"

"Okay King once I find out who did this I will let you know so you can take care of them, but as of now, I'm still trying to find out," Sgt. Moretti said hanging up in King's ear.

"Fuck you, King. I'm about to be the man on these streets," he said to himself.

* * * * *

Erica was chilling in the house with Dawud Jr. watching TV and came across the news on what happened on Pine St. The news broadcaster dubbed it the "Pine Street Massacre."

"They always blowing shit up on the news to make it sound worse than it sounds," Erica said as she blew out the Kush she inhaled. She yelled out to DJ as she put it out.

"Yes mommy," he shouted back as he walked down the steps to see what she wanted.

"Time to go to bed, it's getting late."

"Aww man," he responded just like any kid would that didn't like having to hear those infamous words when they were enjoying their time.

"Don't aww man me. Just do what I said."

"Okay," DJ said while he walked back up stairs.

As soon as he made it back upstairs, Erica's phone started to ring. To the left, to the left blasted out, as she knew not to answer the phone because of the ring tone that was programmed for her baby daddy. After not answering the last five calls from him her phone rung without a ring tone and she knew that was weird because who was calling her that wasn't programmed in her phone, but she answered anyway.

"Hello."

"Yes, Erica. This is Brian from Triple X Productions."

"Okay Brian what's up? You must be calling because you have some good news."

"Yeah that's true, we gone film ya scene soon so get ready."

"Okay Brian I'm digging that. Now Brian, let me ask you what's after this cause my mind is always in the future,"

"I mean all I can tell you is more movies right now, but this is gone be ya first time on camera so you got to get pass the first shot."

"Okay I feel you on that, I got that covered though I have my medicine".

"Wait, hold up medicine? What you mean medicine? You're not some type of basket case, is you?"

"No," Erica said while cracking up at Brian's comment, "Boy I was talking 'bout my Kush."

"Okay cool most girls do have to use before they film. Mow see if you don't first then we go from there, but let me go I'm gone call you back to let you know the location."

"Okay Brian I'll talk to you later," Erica said before hanging up and blazing the rest of her Kush.

* * * * *

Sgt. Moretti arrived at 10th and Wolf where Joey and Johnny were hiding out. They already had put a pound of Kush to the side and began smoking before Frank even arrived.

"What the fuck, I know y'all didn't take one for y'all selves. Don't y'all know that's money y'all smoking?"

"You want to show him or do you want me to show him?" Johnny Capers said.

"What? Show me what? Y'all two potheads smoking my shit that's all I see," Frank said getting furious at the sight of them.

As he was continuing to barrage them with insults Capers got up and went upstairs and came back down with a large gym bag full of money.

"Look at what we did in the last hour or so," Capers said as he came back and dumped the money on the table.

Sgt. Moretti couldn't believe all the money he was staring at.

"How much money am I staring at?"

"You are looking at $25,000. We sold 10 pounds for $2,500. Not bad, huh?" Capers asked.

"Wow! Give me $15,000 and y'all split the rest," Sgt. Moretti commanded. "Now I underestimated y'all so how long it's gone take for y'all to move the other nine."

"Man, I don't know, but we will see," Capers said.

"Well good. When that happens, we are going to hit another house."

"Okay cool," both Johnny and Joey agreed as Sgt. Moretti grabbed his slice of the pie then left them the rest.

* * * * *

"Yo shit is getting real as shit right now y'all. We gotta make the right moves", Chase Money said while him and the Gwap Gang was assembled on 54th and Chestnut.

"Y'all seen the news our connect is being targeted so we got to grind harder with this music shit."

"Yeah I feel you," Banks said. "This street shit isn't promising like that rap money we got coming in."

"I'm glad we on the same page Banks. Now what's up with the rest of y'all?"

Everybody else agreed on what Chase and Banks was saying. Chase then pulled out his cell to hit up Erica to give her the money for the show.

"Hello?" Erica answered like she was sleep.

"What's up Erica? This Chase Money. I'm calling to see if I could drop off that money for the show?'

"What you wanted to come now, Chase?"

"Yeah. As a matter of fact, I could do that right now if that's cool with you."

"Alright I will be waiting outside on my porch, and please bring some Kush with you too."

"How many sacks do you want?"

"The usual two dubs will do for now."

"Cool me and a couple of people from my squad gone be around," Chase said as they hung up.

"Yo Scrilla! Pass me off two dubs good brotha. Yo Banks, Paperboi, walk me around Walnut. Aye Scrilla hold it down with the rest of the fam while we go round her and drop this Kush and paper off."

Before they left Banks and Paperboi, grabbed their hammers that were hidden by the front step trashcans and after grabbing them they tucked them in their pants and were ready to walk round the corner. They never knew when they gone need them especially walking around the corner. They never knew when some shit was going to jump off especially with what transpired on the corner of 56th and Walnut in front of the Chinese restaurant. They ended up walking to the corner of 54th and Walnut until they made a right onto Walnut. They then walked down Walnut until they came between 55th and 56th where Erica was patiently waiting for them on the porch.

"What's up, Erica?" Chase Money said as he passed off a brown paper bag that had the money for the show and a couple of flyers to the show.

"Nothing much Chase, did you bring my Kush?" Erica said while looking in the bag.

"Oh yeah, here" Chase said while passing her two dubs. She then passed him $40, then pulled out a Dutch to proceed to rolling up one.

"Y'all ready for y'all show?" Erica asked while splitting the Dutch.

"Hell Yeah! As you can see, I gave you the money and the flyers."

"Alright cool Chase. I will make sure I pass them out."

"Yeah we gone pass them out and we gone promote it on our Myspace page. We trying to make sure that this shit pops off the way it should."

"That's what's up Chase. I'm glad to see that you are putting the right energy where it needs to be," Erica said as she was finished rolling up her Dutch and started to put the flame to it.

"Hold up y'all. Ain't that da cop car that came up on us when we were on 56th and Spruce?" Chase asked as he peeped out the scene.

"I don't know but it sure does look like it," Banks responded.

"Yo I'm gone check it out," Chase said.

Chase Money walked to the corner of 56th and Walnut to peep the scene, and as he walked up he recognized Sgt. Moretti who was spotted sitting peeping the scene out on the block.

"Let me find out your looking for me Mr., umm hold up you never told me your name officer?"

"You don't need to know my name just get in so we can talk business."

"I don't do business with cops."

Sgt. Moretti pulled out his nine and pointed it at Chase while he was leaning in the window.

"I'm not asking, I'm telling you," Sgt. Moretti said.

Chase walked over to the passenger seat even though he didn't want to because he felt like if he pulled out the nine on him he didn't have the fear to use it.

"So what you want to talk about?" Chase asked as he hopped in.

"I'm about to be the man on these streets and I want you to work for me."

"Yo what are you talking about Mr.?"

"Don't play dumb with me your little team buys Kush off of King?"

"Man I don't know where you getting ya info from, but where do you see us moving Kush at?"

"Okay you playing hard ball with me again. You guys wouldn't have been in the shootout with King's men if that wasn't true. Plus, without me King's men would have knocked y'all out the box so what is it gone be?"

"So now we got to buy our protection? Ain't this a bitch? But just in case I would take this offer how much would it be?"

"Let's see if you buy from me it would be $2,500 a pound."

"Man I get my shit $1,000 a pound from King, what kind of bullshit is that?"

"The extra would be for protection."

"Alright man you got a deal, but you got to do something for me. You got to sponsor my little brother into the academy. He wants to become a cop."

Sgt. Moretti took a deep breath and agreed to the terms since he was gone do business with him the way he wanted.

"Now that we got out the way, how many pounds can you handle?" Sgt. Moretti asked.

"How many you got?" Chase asked.

"Ten right now," Sgt. Moretti answered.

"You got them to pass off right now or I got to wait to get them?"

"Matter of fact here's my card call me tomorrow and I'm gone let you know when we can meet up."

"Alright cool, Sgt. Moretti." Chase said finally getting his name off the card, and then he hopped out Moretti's car then walked up to where Banks, Paperboi, and Erica was still sitting at.

"Yo was that the cop boy?" Paperboi asked.

"Yeah that was him Paperboi, and he talking like he taking over King's operations. Now he wants us to work for him instead of King and he said he gone set up protection when that goes down."

"Now the only question I got for you Chase is do you trust what he said?" Banks said.

"Right now Banks I guess it's the best move we got to survive, but like I said earlier we gone go harder with this rap shit so we can make that transition."

"Good luck and here I know you need this right now," Erica said passing Chase Money the second Dutch she rolled and blazed up.

"Yeah you read my mind," Chase said while taking the Dutch and inhaling deeply.

Homicide City

Chapter 7

Detective Patterson decided to get him some morning pussy, so he called the person that he had on his mind all the time.

"What took you so long?" he asked as he answered his door when she arrived.

"Look I got to get dressed for work too so don't start your bullshit early in the morning."

Detective Patterson just smiled at how the lady talked at him. He didn't mind a little aggression before he got some pussy.

"Well you got me here. What's up with the dick? Am I gone get some or not? I don't like my time to be wasted."

"Cool. Bring your ass over here so I can bend you over on my counter top."

She walked over and lifted up her skirt and pulled down her panties.

"Thanks, but I could've done that," Detective Patterson said while he gave her ass a nice, firm smack.

He then took two fingers and reached over her and started playing with her clit, as this made her pussy get wet the way he wanted it. He then proceeded to put on his Magnum, and then inserted his hard penis.

"Ooh yeah daddy, smack my ass while you fuck me."

Detective Patterson decided to get a little creative and put her in a scissor sex move and put one leg on his shoulder and proceeded to grind inside her sugar walls.

"Natasha you like this dick, don't you?"

"Yes I do, I do keep fucking this pussy, daddy. I have been waiting to see how this dick felt, partner."

"Yeah, well now your wait is over and I'm all in it girl, but I'm 'bout to nut," Patterson said as he started to go in and out faster making her scream his name out.

As he was in the process of ejaculating, he woke up from his wet dream.

"What da fuck?" he said out loud waking up, "Damn, that dream was crazy." Now he had to get up and get ready for the day.

* * * * *

Detective Patterson arrived at the station only to pull up at the same time his partner pulled up.

"Damn. I wonder if I should tell her?" he muttered to himself.

"What's up, Natasha? Are you ready for today, partner?"

"Yes I am always prepared for what's next," she responded.

"Well good cause they should have what we need to prepare for this case."

"Yeah that's what I'm counting on, so we will see."

As soon as they walked in together, Captain Morello pulled them inside his office to give them the rundown on the case.

"Look we got the fingerprints on all the bodies that were found at the scene of the crime. All four came up as illegal immigrants tracing back to their Jamaican roots. So if we find out who they are connected to, we could solve this case."

"Captain now that you say that I can only think of one man that has the money and the power to do so, and he goes by the name King on the streets. Now me and Natasha can go investigate him."

"Good put that on the agenda for today, because if that is true, then the evidence is pointing straight at him and we can build a strong case against him."

"Oh and Captain please don't let this info leak into the department we don't need anybody covering up anything if we want to solve this case."

"Here we go with the corrupt cop issue you keep having."

"Listen. It's not an issue. I'm gone be the one to say it again, I smell a rat in the department and I'm gone lead you to him."

"Okay Patterson. Just get what I need and what I need is a solved case on these bodies."

"Okay sir me and Richmond will get on that ASAP. Let's go partner. Let's go do what we do best," Patterson said as they got up and left his office.

As they left the office and went to their desks and sat down, Sgt. Moretti came over to talk shit.

"Hey look at what we have here, Magnum and Lacey," Moretti said jokingly, "Do y'all get it? Magnum and Lacey since he's always trying to fuck somebody's girl or wife with his favorite condom the Magnum."

"Well I don't need a Magnum when I'm fucking your wife in the ass," Patterson said making a snappy come back.

The officers that were standing around for the barrage of jokes all chimed in like cheerleaders with a loud 'ooh!' After the loud 'ooh' Patterson and Richmond gave each other a high five for Patterson's snappy comeback.

"Could you please get away from us with your breath smelling like a pound of ten day old mozzarella?" Detective Richmond added, coming to the aid of her partner.

"Bitch wasn't nobody talking to you," Sgt. Moretti said.

"Bitch? I got ya bitch right here," Richmond said as she reached for her nine.

"Oh let me step back. I forgot about you, sharpshooter. Watch out guys we got a loose cannon on the force," Moretti said while making his cheerleaders on the side laugh.

Captain Morello stepped out his office and put an end to the comedy showcase between his workers.

"Hey I'm not paying y'all to congregate, and insult each other now get to work before I start handing out pink slips!"

Everybody went their separate ways except Moretti he stayed to parlay with Patterson and Richmond to try and pry into the case.

"Hey how's the case coming along guys?"

"That's none of your business. Don't come over her snooping around after insulting us."

"Well don't take it so personal. That was just jokes, but I was trying to find out cause I have a lead for y'all. His name is Chase Money and he runs this little gang called the Gwap Gang, they perpetrate like they run a music company but they are connected to the streets too, and let me tell you they have the man power to do what was done on Pine St."

"Thanks for the lead Sgt., now we gone make sure we check that out," Patterson told Moretti as he walked away.

"I don't believe him, he's seems like a slimy bastard," Detective Richmond said.

"Well why do you think I always say I smell a rat partner? I know it sounds crazy but I think we just found him."

* * * * *

King and Tony Moretti were having a sit down at Studio 7 and Tony wanted the sit down to be on mutual grounds just in case something went down but King told him when it comes down to business he's not a violent man, he's only about business.

"So King, when can I receive my merchandise?"

"Well as of now I'm not making no large moves until I find out who hit me house."

"What's that got to do with our business arrangements?"

"Well how do I know if it wasn't you that hit me house?"

"Because you were going to give me twenty pounds of your Kush product at a thousand a pound. Now you grow it yourself so any profit you make is a great profit now ask yourself why would I destroy that type of business when we all can profit?"

"Greed brethren greed. You guys are always moving off of greed."

"Well to tell you the truth I think you should take a look inside your family because you guys don't know the code of loyalty."

"Me don't care what you bumbaclot tink bout me, me men know not to double cross the King."

"Okay King whatever you say, but all I know is I'm ready to make this move with you now you told us you would have twenty pounds now we are here for business not to insult each other."

"Okay give me more time to tink bout it brethren."

"Okay I will give you more time to think on it, but let me just tell you it wasn't none of my men that hit your house because if it was they would be floating in a fucking river by now fucking up my business. But I see where you stand and I respect that," Tony said as he shook King's hand and got up to leave.

As they were leaving, Detective Patterson and Richmond were pulling up.

"Wow this is interesting. What the hell is Moretti doing coming out of King's place of business?" Detective Patterson said as he and Richmond observed.

"So hold up Moretti, is this the guy you say Sgt. Moretti is connected with?" Detective Richmond asked.

"Yup that's Tony Moretti, he makes illegal moves but he's mister untouchable. His peoples are the ones that make the transactions so when any department tries to make anything stick to this man his people takes the fall."

"Wow, yeah that's what I call a real Mr. Untouchable," Richmond commented.

"Yeah but now I'm thinking why is he coming out of King's place of business?"

"Well partner that's why we are here to see just that," Detective Richmond said as they both got out of the car and walked into the restaurant part of the business.

As they walked in a couple of King's men were sitting in the restaurant part of the establishment, as they were all staring at Detective

Richmond. One of the men were boldly enough to speak to her.

"Finally, I meet my queen," the knotty dread said.

"I'm not your fucking queen, now where's ya boss at?" Detective Richmond said as she showed her badge.

The man put his hands up to gesture he was out of order.

"My bad respect, respect."

"Now that we got that out of the way where's King?" Detective Patterson said joining in.

"There's no 1 King here, we all King's brethren," the man said as he stood up to try and show his manhood.

Detective Patterson quickly kneed him in his nut sack and took his manhood away from him.

"Now I'm only gone ask once more. Where's King?"

King stepped out of his office and kindly greeted Detective Patterson and Richmond.

"Welcome to my place of business, detectives. How can I be of service today?"

"Well you can start by telling ya man that I'm not to be fucked with," Detective Patterson said while looking at the man on the ground still holding his nuts.

"Everybody cool. Show respect for the detectives. Now, once again, what brings you here today?"

"Four bodies. Now, let's talk privately."

All three of them walked into King's office to talk.

"Dam that's all you Jamaicans do is smoke weed huh?" Detective Patterson asked.

"Helps relieve the stress brethren, now you're not gone lock me up for this, are you?"

"No we are here for the bodies King. Now let's talk."

After King knew he had the green light he blazed up a fat spliff.

"Bold move King." Detective Patterson said while getting a cloud of Kush blown in his face, "Now King the four dead Jamaicans, tell me about that."

"You come here to tell me about four dead men I have no ties to, how about you show some respect, detective?"

"Well how did they get over here without the proper paper work King? You're the only man I know that can make that happen round these parts."

"Oh you think that cause of me power I have that I can make that possible. Well you're wrong. I do things the legal way now, brethren. You think that I like having people like you come to my place of business and interrogate me? I'm the King!"

"Okay King no need to raise your voice or get bent out of shape, but I know you're connected to these bodies and I'm gone find out what you're not telling me."

King just turned his chair around and gave Patterson and Richmond his back while finishing his spliff signaling the conversation was over. Patterson and Richmond looked at each other baffled at first then they just got up and left the office. As they walked out another one of King's men decided to be bold with Detective Richmond and grabbed her nicely round ass as she walked by. Her reaction was a quick elbow to his forehead that knocked him from the chair he was sitting in onto the floor.

"Anybody else wanna touch?" Richmond yelled out. No one answered.

"Disrespectful ass Jamaicans!" Detective Richmond complained as they walked outside and hopped in the car.

"Listen partner let me ask you this, that aroma in there wasn't that familiar to you?" Detective Patterson asked.

"No. I wasn't paying it any attention like that."

"That same aroma was in the house when we was checking it out, and that's the same aroma that was in King's office now. I know he's tied in this somehow."

"Good work partner now do we go back in and bust him for the weed?"

"No we just gone let the chips fall where they fall. And let them keep exposing themselves," Detective Patterson answered as he drove off.

Meanwhile King was still in his office enjoying the rest of his spliff, as he pulled out his cell phone to make an important call.

"Moretti, you have two detectives coming by to see me. I don't need any heat on me now get rid of them."

"Okay King. You got it," Sgt. Moretti said as he hung up knowing it was Detective Patterson and Richmond.

Homicide City

Chapter 8

"So where are you two at with the case?" Captain Morello asked while Detective Patterson and Richmond were in his office.

"Well let me break it down boss, we know them bodies is connected to King. We went to go and talk to him to get the answers but you know how the gangsters play then don't really open up the way we want. Now when we arrived guess who was walking out?"

"Who?" Captain Morello asked Patterson.

"The infamous Tony Moretti."

Captain Morello just took a deep breath knowing how untouchable this man was.

"You mean he was in the heart of West Philly with this man they call King?"

"Yes. Richmond and I witnessed this with our own eyes, Captain. Now I think whatever King has or can offer Moretti wants, but I know for a fact that he's not gone touch it because of his mastermind."

"Yeah so this what I want you guys to do. I want you two to find out why."

"Okay now, Captain, you know this is gone get dirty, right?"

"I don't care how dirty it gets. They are not gone have these streets upside down."

"Okay captain but let me ask you this. Did Sgt. Moretti come to you about another lead called the Gwap Gang?"

"No he never told me anything about a gang called Gwap Gang or whoever they are. What is that? Some street slang?"

"I don't know but I figure that could be another lead, and also you don't think that he is connected with Tony Moretti?"

Captain Morello just stared at Patterson with a blank look as if to say this is not the time.

"What captain listen I have a bad feeling about that guy and you already know this, and I'm usually not a bad judge of character."

"Just solve the case before it gets worse, and you let me worry about my workers."

"Sir, can I just add that I think it's true too?"

"Detective Richmond if I wanted your opinion I would have asked."

"Sorry, sir."

"Now the two of you need to focus on Tony and King and try to keep an close eye on their movements cause those bodies didn't drop for nothing."

Patterson and Richmond both walked out the office to get on with their duties for the day.

"Why do he get so offended when we bring up other officers?" Richmond asked.

"He defended me the same way when everybody was saying I was fucking everybody's wives and girlfriends, so in turn that's how he is he defends his officers until the truth is revealed."

"I understand, partner. I wouldn't have it no other way. He's a loyal captain."

* * * * *

"I'm loving you guys right now," Sgt. Moretti said as he gave both Johnny Capers and Joey Five Fingers kisses on the cheek.

"Hey save the kisses. I think kissing another man is so gay! I don't even like when Tony does it," Johnny said while wiping his cheek.

"I'm just excited how you guys are moving and hustling for me that's all, I mean you guys made it up to my salary as a cop in two days."

"I think the product is speaking for itself," Joey said.

"Yeah Joey, I know, and that's why it's time to get our hands on some more of this product. Are you guys down for another heist, Caper?"

"Hell yeah we down. You know Caper is my middle name?" Johnny said speaking up for the both of them.

"Good cause we doing one soon, but at the moment I have another job for you two," Sgt. Moretti said as he pulled out the evidence, "Now this job is very touchy but it has to be done."

"Cool. We down," they both said.

"Okay then. This is how it needs to be handled," Moretti said getting into the scheme of things.

* * * * *

113

Detective Patterson took his partner to get a cheese steak at one of his favorite places to go, Max's on Broad and Erie.

"Now this is the hood favorite. One day, I will take you to South Philly to Geno's but the hood we come to Max's," Patterson explained as they hopped out his car.

"What's this area called?" Detective Richmond asked being inquisitive on where the place was located.

"This here is North Philly. Temple College is not too far away on Broad St."

"Wow is it always this much people out here like this? I mean what do people do around here?"

"Yeah it's a lot of traffic but all I'm gone tell you is that it goes down around here as you can see."

They walked to the corner of Broad and Erie and walked inside Max's, and had no trouble ordering since it wasn't a lot of customers at the time.

"Yes sir can I get a half chicken cheese steak with fried onions, ketchup, lettuce, and tomatoes? What you gone order partner?"

"Ugh, let me get the same thing that sounds so good you gone have me getting fat fucking around with you."

"Umm that's too late. You haven't been looking in the mirror lately," Patterson said jokingly.

"Hey don't be commented on my thickness! I look and feel good."

"Okay. So I found your Achilles heel!"

"Yeah, you can say that my weight is my weakness sort of but I keeps it under control. I don't let it get out of hand to where I'm insecure."

"Okay cool. Whatever you say," Patterson answered while they were in the process of waiting for their steaks to be finished.

A few minutes later, their steaks were wrapped up and ready to go.

"They smell good," Richmond said as they paid for them and walked out.

As soon as they got in the car Patterson unwrapped his and took a nice size bite.

"Damn, partner. You couldn't wait, huh?"

"Hell no! First of all, I'm hungry as shit and I always take that first bite like this to take away the hunger pains."

"Well don't tell me you gone eat and drive at the same time!"

"Yes and I'm gone show you how we do up in Philly. I'm gone put it in my lap and take bites while I drive."

"All I know is you better pay attention to the road and not that damn sandwich while I'm in this car!"

"Don't be so paranoid! I got this." Patterson said as his pulled off and drove up to get on highway 76.

As he got on 76, there were a couple of cars behind him waiting to get on along with him blowing their horns impatiently. He finally made the left to get on and they were on the way back to West Philly.

"I'm gone take you past the zoo while we are out," Patterson said.

"Okay. Cool with me," Richmond said.

Patterson took a quick bite of his cheese steak and swerved a little in the process of trying to eat and drive on the highway at the same time.

"See look at you, bout to cause an accident trying to be greedy and shit!"

"Man we ain't getting into no accidents! I told you I got this!"

They were half a mile away from the Girard Exit, so he reared off into the right lane, as he got into the lane he decided to take another bite of his cheese steak. As he bit into the sandwich, bullets started to come through the car shattering both the driver and passenger seat window. The incident caused him to swerve off to the side of the road.

"Oh shit! What the fuck? Did you get to see who did that?" Patterson asked all out of breath from what just occurred.

"No, I was too busy with making sure you didn't crash."

"Damn! You're bleeding," Patterson said as he examined her wound from the shattering of the glass. Her arm was badly banged up.

"Somebody put a hit out on us! You think it was Tony Moretti?"

"I don't know partner, but whoever it is was almost accomplished what they were out to do."

As they were talking, a highway patrol officer pulled up behind them.

"Look let me do the talking Richmond so we won't be on this dam highway all day night,"

"Is everything okay with you guys?" the officer asked as he walked up on Patterson's car.

"Well we are detectives, and we just got shot at and ran off the road but we are okay."

"Well it seems to me that you two are in need of medical. You guys are cut from the glass."

"Yeah we know but it's not that bad. I still can drive to my destination then seek help."

"Well how are you gone do that with two flat tires?" the officer asked sounding like he was being a smart ass.

"Shit, well I got my AAA card. Never leave home without it. Plus I'm gone call my Captain and alert him to what happened."

Patterson pulled out his cell and made the call.

"Captain look we ran into a little situation on 76. Somebody done shot us off the road I. think it was a hit put out on me and my partner."

"What? How do you know it was a hit and not one of your crazy stalkers?"

"Not now Captain! We sitting on the side of the road waiting for an ambulance and AAA."

"Wait ambulance, don't tell me one of you guys got hit, please don't tell me that!"

"No Captain, we didn't get hit. We just got cut from the shattering of my two front windows. Must have been amateurs."

"Well when you guys are done with that, bring y'all ass back to the station and I mean straight to the station."

The ambulance arrived on the scene ten minutes later to bandage them up and make sure they were no more injuries made within the incident. AAA arrived a few minutes after to change the flat tires and in no time they were on their way back to the station.

As they walked in Sgt. Moretti was the first to spot them coming in as he spoke.

"Damn! What happened to y'all two?"

"We were involved in an alley fight with stray cats," Patterson said making a joke out of the incident.

"Well fuck you too, Patterson. I was making sure y'all was cool."

Captain Morello came out of his office and called them into the office. When they got situated inside he closed the door and even shut the blinds to signify that he wanted to keep this between the three of them.

"So before we get started let me ask the both of you this, with this incident that occurred do I have to pull y'all off this case for any reason?"

"I'm good Captain. I'm always prepared to get a little dirty," Richmond answered.

"Hell no, Captain! You ain't pulling us off this case, I think we are on to something," Patterson answered as Morello shook his head knowing he was gone get a crazy response out of Patterson.

Homicide City

Chapter 9

"Okay action," Brian said on the set of him filming the scene with Erica and her co-star in the scene Mandingo.

"Yes may I help you sir?"

"Yes you can I think I have the flu."

"Are you sure? I mean you are little hot maybe it's because of me that your hot and not the flu?"

"Its only one way to find out Ms. Silk-E."

"Well you're right its only one way to find out Mandingo."

"Okay cut, that was great Erica good way to drag him into the sex scene. Now Mandingo get that penis hard so we can start filming the oral shots then we gone go to the cum shot scene."

They started filming the oral shot as Erica was enjoying the oral she was giving Mandingo until he started ramming her mouth. As he started ramming his dick in her mouth, it instantly starting bringing pain to her jaws.

"Okay cut! Good work, Mandingo. I hope you ready for the cum shot scene."

"Yeah, just about."

"Well shit! Let's wait a minute let me get my jaws ready," Erica said while massaging them.

"Okay now I'm ready," she said a couple of minutes later.

"Okay she's ready now action!"

Mandingo got straight into the role again but this time he didn't have any mercy on Erica's mouth. He started ramming her throat to the point she started gagging. Three minutes later, he pulled out of her mouth and squirted all over her face.

"Cut, good cum shot Mandingo!" Brian said as they were complete with Erica's first scene as a porn star.

"All right Erica you can go get clean! We are officially done, and good job on your first scene!"

Erica couldn't feel any better with hearing those words. She thought that she was going to throw up on Mandingo's dick during the scene from how she was gagging. He made tears come to her eyes, and she wasn't humiliated by being squirted on during the cum shot. It was just how hard he was ramming that she didn't like. She hopped in the shower really quickly to get fresh for a quick five minutes then she was cool. Mandingo was waiting for her to come back out she peeped as she came out.

"What are doing? I know you ain't waiting for me, are you?"

"As a matter of fact, I was hoping that we could go get something to eat and maybe a drink after."

"Okay that's cool with me. You don't seem like a stalker," Erica said as her comment made them both laugh.

"Now I was thinking Fridays on the Parkway. Is that cool with you, Erica?"

"That sounds great! Now, are you treating me?"

"Yeah why not? I mean after the way I treated your mouth a minute ago I should just go ahead and treat you to dinner."

"Yeah you do have a point there Mandingo. You did murder my mouth."

* * * * *

Erica and Mandingo were enjoying their dinner date at Fridays. Mandingo ordered the shrimp Alfredo with a glass of wine while Erica ordered the grilled chicken with cheese with grilled vegetables, baked potato, and a glass of wine.

"Are you enjoying your meal Erica?" Mandingo asked sparking conversation.

"Yes I am, thanks for asking."

"Now that we are getting into conversation let me ask you Erica, what made you get into porn?"

"Well I strip, so my boss gave me the card that Brian gave him since Brian was interested in me so I took on the job."

"Yeah the strip clubs are his favorite spot to recruit. He already knows y'all are hungry."

"I am hungry. I'm a hustler that's not scared to get money."

"But let me tell you Erica it's a rough business, you might get asked to do things you're not used to doing."

123

"Well I'm prepared to. Believe me when I tell you."

"Well let me tell you my story. I'm a model but things got slow for me and one day I came across Brian and he proposed that I get into porn. I get $1,000 a scene, but one day he wanted me to anal fuck this broad, that went against my morals cause I don't do that but that $1,000 made me do it. That shit was nasty my dick was browner than it was before I did it."

"Ill, I'm eating here and you talking about anal sex."

"Well I'm sorry but I'm just keeping it real with you. You might get asked to do something out of the ordinary."

"I understand completely."

"Now I'm a God-fearing man, but when my money got low I had to bite the bullet but I'm hoping modeling opens back up for me."

"That's a good way to look at things Mandingo, and I hope everything works out for you."

"It's a little rough now since the agencies found out I do porn so they turn away like they don't even watch porn."

"Damn that's fucked up. Hypocrites always do that like they perfect."

"Yeah it's cool though cause I'm doing bout two movies a month with Brian, and on top of that I travel to L.A. and do five movies when I go over on the west coast at about $2,500 a movie."

"Wow! Get that money, Mandingo."

"Yeah I stay on my grind, then last time I was out L.A. this video producer wanted me to be in his R&B videos at $5,000 a video."

"Wow that's what's up! I'm supposed to be in a video myself."

"For real, Erica? I see we have a lot in common."

"Yeah we do. Even my dad raised me to be a God-fearing woman but I hit rock bottom fucking with a good for nothing baby father so I got into stripping but the sky's the limit with me I know I'm not gone be doing this forever."

"So now that we are done eating let's get out of here and go burn this food off I know a couple of places we can go dance at."

"Where you taking me?" Mandingo asked.

"What type of places you like to go to?"

"I like all types of clubs reggae, hip hop it doesn't matter."

"Cool I know a place around my way called Studio 7, it's a reggae bar but it be popping."

"Alright cool. Let's be out," Mandingo said as he paid the bill and they left to go to Studio 7.

* * * * *

When they arrived at Studio 7. the place was packed wall-to-wall and jumping. All the girls were winding and grinding on the pelvises of the men to the music that was blasting out of the speakers.

"Yeah this my type of place," Mandingo said as he had to talk directly into Erica's ear because the music was so loud. "Erica I'm about to order a beer you want anything?"

"Yes, you can get me a sex on the beach."

"Let me get a sex on the beach and a corona," Mandingo said to the barmaid.

"That'll be $9.50," the barmaid said with her strong Jamaican accent.

Mandingo passed off a dub and told her to keep the change.

"Okay balla, I saw that," Erica said peeping out how he told her to keep the change.

Erica's drink tasted like Kool-Aid as she guzzled the first one down in ten minutes, so she ordered another one.

"You better take it easy. I heard them type of drinks creep up on ya."

"I will be alright," Erica said as she stood up. The alcohol started to take effect as she caught her balance and started to dance to the bass of the beats popping her ass towards Mandingo as he sat on a barstool by the bar. Mandingo enjoyed all the ass that was grinding on his dick as it made him erect. Erica started smiling at him as she felt it, as she already knew how he felt inside her mouth, but she was ready to feel him in her sugar walls. She leaned back to speak in his ear and whisper her sexual thoughts.

"You want to come to my house and enjoy some of this pussy, Mandingo?"

"I thought you would never ask, but hell yeah."

"Well let's not stop dancing just yet my pussy is getting nice and warm for you."

"Okay. I know you feel my pole rising inside my pants, don't you?" Mandingo said as they both started to laugh.

After another sex on the beach and three more songs, Erica was ready to feel the dick she was grinding on.

"C'mon let's go," Erica commanded grabbing Mandingo by the arm.

"You good enough to drive Erica?"

"Yeah I'm straight. We only got a couple of blocks to go I live right around the corner."

"Okay I was just making sure," Mandingo said as they walked to their cars.

She hopped in her car and waited for him to make sure he was ready. Once she saw him pull up, she pulled off and proceeded to her house. She drove up 55th and Chestnut made a right, and then drove straight to Walnut made and made a right onto Walnut. Mandingo pulled in the first parking space he saw that was closer to 55th St. as she pulled in her parking space in front of her house. She saw in her rearview that he was already parked, so she hopped out and waited till he got out and started walking up to her house. By the time she made it to the door, Mandingo was behind her rubbing her ass. This made Erica anxious as she got the door open and went straight for the couch. She started taking off her clothes as Mandingo moved in unison. It only took bout to minutes for them to be naked as they started to kissing and licking each other. Erica took Mandingo's hand so could feel the warmth and wetness of her pussy.

"You feel that?" she asked while he rubbed and started to finger her.

Mandingo stopped and guided her head straight to his penis, but Erica had other plans. She flipped on his lap into a 69 position and put her pussy on his mouth as she proceeded to give him head.

"Oh damn," Mandingo said as he was intrigued by the move Erica made.

After giving each other oral for a good ten minutes, Erica was ready for some dick action. So she got up and asked him to put on a condom. He was already prepared as he went inside his pants and pulled out a XL Magnum and put it on. After putting it on Erica hopped on his dick and started riding him with her back facing him and her hands touching the floor.

"Damn," Mandingo said at the sight of her ass going up and down.

After five minutes of that she got up and put her titties in his mouth and got back on his dick to ride him again.

"Oh my God! I can feel ya dick inside my stomach!" Erica said as she took all of it in.

Erica started grinding on it back and forth until she climaxed.

"Oh my God!" she let out as she started shaking while riding his dick. She didn't stop she just kept going as she was about to cum back to back.

"Oh my God! I'm about to cum again! Goddamn, Mandingo! Ya dick is so good."

If her neighbors didn't know his name, they would have known it now the way she was yelling it out. Mandingo decided to show her what he was about as he lifted her up as he stood up and started fucking her standing up.

"Oh my God Mandingo you gone fuck me like this? Goddamn."

He started out by walking around in a small circle, until he felt that he was about to cum. He then laid her on her back and pulled her legs wide apart and gave her the jackhammer move until he busted his nut.

"Goddamn, nigga! You was fucking the shit out of me!" Erica said after the session.

She then got up and looked in her ashtray to see if she left something to smoke on. As she looked she seen a nice piece of a Dutch she put out, so she grabbed it and lit it up.

"You smoke weed, Mandingo?"

"No I don't smoke but you don't mind if I leave, do you?"

"No I don't mind at all," Erica said lying to herself and Mandingo, because deep down, she wanted more sex.

Mandingo stood up and got dressed and was out the door in less than five minutes. As he walked to his car two people ran up on him snatched his car keys and threw him in his backseat.

Chapter 10

"Yo this shit gone be crazy y'all," Chase Money said speaking into the camera while the Gwap Gang was recording their documentary.

"We bout to take y'all on a quick adventure to the Gwap Gang crib, then we gone have a nice peep show with a couple of freak jawns getting naked all types of shit is gone be going down tonight, hold up y'all my phone ringing. What's up Tanya you and ya homies still coming to the crib right? Alright cool see y'all when y'all get there, Yeah world I'm back that was the girls that's gone be there so its official it's going down the official Gwap Gang Bash real nigga style".

Scrilla who was the one filming the documentary while they were walking started to pay attention to this car that was easing in the background. He didn't know what was about to go down so he stopped recording.

"Yo what the fuck Scrilla? I wasn't finished I was just getting into the zone," Chase said not knowing why he stopped recording.

Scrilla pointed out the car that was creeping up on them as everybody got into war mode.

Banks and Scrilla were the only ones packing at the time so they let everybody else fall back. They walked past the car on 56th and Chestnut as they were on their way walking up towards 55th by the Dunkin Donuts. Still the car was just sitting there like the people inside were scheming. Then that's when the back window started to roll down slowly, and Banks and Scrilla reacted in orderly fashion unloading their nines as this made the car speed off.

The Gwap Gang ran through the parking lot of Dunkin Donuts up to Sansom St. Everybody stopped to catch their breath, as Banks was the first to speak on the incident.

"Yo niggas is haters. I wonder why they was creeping like that, I didn't even want to let off on them niggas like that but when that window started to roll down I said fuck it and let 'em have it!"

"Yeah that's what made me squeeze off too," Scrilla added.

"Well the good thing is nobody got hit on our behalf. I don't know about them niggas but fuck it. They deserve to get hit doing dumb shit like that. All I know is we good so let's get back to the crib and get ready to fuck with some bitches. Yo now I wish we would've got that on tape, we could've been like on that Menace 2 Society shit and keep rewinding it back and forth laughing how y'all blasted on them niggas," Chase said while they were walking to the crib.

* * * * *

The doorbell rang to the Gwap Gang hideout as Chase sent Paperboi to let in Tanya and her homies. Chase was busy setting up the camera for their little party as they walked in. Tanya being the vocal one out the group went straight for her favorite Gwap Gang representative Chase Money and gave him a kiss on the cheek and a tight hug,

"Now who do we have here?" Chase asked talking about her four homies she brought with her.

"Here we have my four closes friends, Cashmere, Amina, Camaya, and Salita," Tanya said pointing each one out individually.

"Banks, Paperboi, Scrilla, Stacks, as you can see we bout to have a ball, but ladies let me tell y'all me and my squad got a thousand a piece so we bout to make it thunderstorm in here."

The girls didn't need to hear no more they ran upstairs to change into more seductive clothing and came back within minutes with their individual outfits they picked out for the occasion. Chase Money turned the camera on and spoke into it.

"This here is for the 18 and older crowd, if you ain't of age you don't need to be watching this."

After he finished, he laughed into the camera amusing his self as Banks threw on a mix tape that started out with USDA blasting out "Throw This Money." As soon as the girls heard that pop through the speakers they started shaking their asses and Banks was the first one to throw his first 100 ones in the air.

"Yo Banks spark that Kush up dog!" Paperboi yelled out.

Cashmere and Amina had the floor on lock with Banks and Paperboi, Camaya and Salita grabbed Stacks and Scrilla and threw them on the couch and gave them personal lap dances. Meanwhile Chase Money was pinned to the wall as Tanya ass had him stuck, while she had her hands on the floor and her ass in the air. Chase was enjoying every bit of the ass show singing along with USDA. He stopped for a quick minute and went into the kitchen to grab bottles of Moet as he passed them out to his squad then went up to the camera again to talk shit.

"You see this? Read my shirt. Gwap Gang we getting money over here and we enjoying life as you should."

As he turned around to go back to party with Tanya she walked up on him naked to take him upstairs.

"Hold up baby, yo who got a lighter before I go upstairs?" Chase yelled out as Banks passed him a lighter so he could spark his Kush up.

After he sparked, he was ready to go upstairs with Tanya. He had his bottle of Moet in one hand and in the other his Kush as they went to the master bedroom. He gave her the bottle to sip on as he took a couple of puffs of his Dutch. She passed him the bottle back and he took a couple of sips, then he turned the Dutch around in his mouth and brought her close to him as he blew it in her mouth as she inhaled. She started to cough from the Kush, so she took the bottle from him to cool down her throat. Tanya was already in horny mode and she couldn't wait to fuck so she started to peel off Chase's Rock and Republic jeans.

"That's what I'm talking 'bout," Chase said as he put the bottle down and kept his Kush burning.

He knew he was about to receive a nice sloppy dick suck so he could sit back smoke and enjoy it.

Now downstairs, it was going down, the rest of the Gwap Gang had it popping. It was over $2,000 on the ground as they had all of the girls shaking their ass on the floor to Juvenile's "Back That Ass Up."

* * * * *

But you know what they say, when you're enjoying life the way they were around the corner there's your enemy trying to bring you down and that's what Sgt. Moretti had in store for them. Sgt. Moretti and his two-man squad Joey Five Fingers and Johnny Capers were busy knocking off another one of King's houses. This house was located on a small block called Felton St. between 62nd and Locust. All they did was tie up the four workers and take another twenty pounds of Kush. The whole thing about the robbery was Sgt. Moretti knew in the back of his mind he was gone call King on this one and say it was the Gwap Gang that did the heists plus he was going to sell the Gwap Gang the Kush. Sgt. Moretti was a snake like that and didn't give two shits about it. He just kept his mind on making money outside of getting his precinct check.

"Listen this how we gone do this, I'm gone pop off a couple of shots in the air. Y'all gone peel off and I'm gone turn my siren on like I pulled up on the robbery," Sgt. Moretti said explaining the situation to Joey and Johnny.

They didn't understand what he was doing but they just went along with the plans as they were gone get their share of the money. After busting his gun in the air Joey and Johnny peeled off and Sgt. Moretti pulled out his cell phone and called King while his police lights were left on so nobody wouldn't call the police.

"King I was riding around and I stumbled upon the culprits that have been robbing you as they were robbing another one of your houses. Now I don't know if you're familiar with them but I found out it was The Gwap Gang."

"Yeah I know Chase Money. He's a one of my best customers that disloyal motherfucker. I got something for him. Good work Moretti, I owe you. Now how about when you finish over there you stop past and I pay you for your services."

"Okay let me clean up this scene and I will stop past."

* * * * *

"Good job Moretti. I don't believe them disloyal niggas. I fed them niggas and this is how they repay the King,"

"Check this out King. This is where you can get them," Moretti said as he passed King one of the Gwap Gang's flyer for their show.

"Good work Moretti! I'm definitely gone set something up for that. I got to get some real shottas to erase these niggas off the earth. But here's five grand for putting in that work and plus I got another surprise. I know how much you would like to fuck some Jamaican pussy so I got some for you."

After King spoke to Moretti he called for Hot Tottie to the room where they were talking. Hot Tottie was what niggas in the hood call an Amazon, she was 6'2", 180 and her ass stuck out like a hatchback. Her lips were full and luscious and she had a pair of D-cups that a newborn would fall in love with. As she entered the room, King left so Hot Tottie and Moretti could get better acquainted. She had on an all black fitted outfit that she took off by the straps as she took it off her titties popped out one by one. Moretti stood in place shocked that her titties were that big.

"Are they real?" Moretti asked at the sight of them.

"Yes they are real, you can feel them," Hot Tottie suggested.

Moretti stuck his hands out and caressed both her titties at the same time, then proceeded to suck her brown supple nipples that when they got hard they were shaped like missiles. After caressing and sucking them he took out his personal cell phone and took a pic of her titties.

"I'm sorry I had to take a pic of those titties they are so perfect."

"No need to apologize, sir."

After he took the picture, she pulled out his dick and started to give him the best blowjob he

137

ever had. Her lips looked like they were permanently swollen so Sgt. Moretti was amazed from the dick suck he was receiving. Hot Tottie squatted down in front of him and got more leverage and started using no hands as she used her hands to play with her nipples and titties. This made Sgt. Moretti so excited he bust in her mouth no less than five minutes draining every little piece of energy he could think his body stored at the time. After she was done, he thought to his self that he wanted to fuck her but he didn't even have the energy to do, so he just got himself together and left.

* * * * *

Erica woke up to go to the bathroom, and after she was done a couple of people were walking past her home speaking loudly so she went to see who they were. It was nobody she knew so she decided to go back to bed. But something strange caught her eye. Mandingo's car was still parked in the same spot. She quickly threw on some sweat pants and a t-shirt and sneaks knowing he was supposed have been left. She then ran outside and approached his Camaro and took a peek inside. After she was done peaking she let out the loudest scream that anybody could imagine from the most horrific sight she ever seen in her existence.

T. Real

Homicide City

Chapter 11

The camera flashed on the sight of Mandingo stuffed in the back seat of his car, his penis was left in his mouth along with his genitals. The scene was gruesome. Erica was traumatized. She was sitting on the step just looking at the ground face dry from all the tears she let out, throat was on fire from screaming at the top of her lungs. Detective Patterson and Richmond decided to get her together so they could ask her a few questions on what transpired.

"Okay ma'am. Could you give me a description of what happened between you and the victim?" Detective Patterson asked.

"Okay I was in a movie scene with him. That's how I met him," Erica began to explain before Detective Patterson cut her off.

"Okay what type of movie would that might be Erica?"

Erica felt a little embarrassed and got quiet for a minute.

"Do you need some quick counseling?" Detective Richmond asked.

"No. I'm okay. My dad does my counseling, and he should be here any minute because I called him before you two showed up."

"Okay since you don't need any counseling, let's get back to your story," Detective Patterson said.

"Okay I'm ready now. I just got into porn. The man that's dead...he was my first scene. We went out and had a couple of drinks and made it back to my house and now he's dead."

"Okay ma'am, you don't have to tell us anymore but let me ask you this. Are you in any danger or did anybody follow you two?"

"No I'm not in any danger that I know of, and we were a little intoxicated so I wouldn't know if we were followed."

"I'm sorry. I know that we should have asked you this before we started but what is your name please?"

"My name is Erica Williams."

"Okay thank you Ms. Williams, now what's the victim's name?"

"I only know him by Mandingo."

"Okay do you have any way of getting his name for me?"

"Yes. I can call my movie producer. He should know."

"Good but hold up did we meet before? I mean this is off the record Erica but I think we have met before."

"I'm sorry sir but I don't remember you from anywhere."

Detective Patterson just sat back and thought about where he saw this beautiful lady.

"That's where its coming together you were coming out of Bishop Lamont Williams Ministries building, now I know your last name is Williams what's the relation?"

"He's my father, sir."

"Oh that explains it, I'm sorry for disrespecting you that day. That's just one of my personalities I'm working on."

"Apology accepted sir, but my dad is gone have a field day with this situation cause he told me not to go further down this path and I did it anyway."

"Yeah I heard about your dad he's like a psychic right?"

"No he's a prophet that can talk to you about your life. He's a great man and well respected in the community."

"Yeah I need to meet your dad," Detective Patterson said.

"Well here's your chance young man," Bishop Williams said as he walked inside.

Erica jumped up and hugged her father at the sight of seeing him, as Detective Patterson and Richmond both greeted him as well.

"Detective, what's going on at my daughter's house?"

"Well sorry to be the bearer of bad news but ya daughter is connected to a body that's outside and we are here asking her the proper questions we need to ask."

Bishop Williams just turned and looked at his daughter and gave her the look of as if he was saying I told you so.

"Now detectives, did my daughter have anything to do with this homicide?"

"No as of right now she is not a suspect and hopefully she won't fall into that category. And let me tell you I don't think she will be from what we heard"

"Well good that makes me feel a whole lot better. Now, is this interview done?"

"Yes here's my card Erica and if you have any more leads, I need you to call me," Detective Patterson said as he and Detective Richmond was getting ready to leave.

As they were about to leave Bishop Williams stopped them in their tracks.

"Excuse me detectives, but I think the both of you need to come and see me. I feel your souls talking to me since you are in my presence and I think it would be beneficial to you."

"Okay. We will follow up with you, sir," Detective Patterson acknowledged.

"My doors are always open people," Bishop Williams said as they left.

"Wasn't that weird Richmond?" Patterson said talking but what he told them.

"Hell yeah gave me the shivers," Detective Richmond commented.

"Hey before y'all take that body fingerprint it and check the car for fingerprints we got to solve this case," Detective Patterson said as they left to go to the precinct.

* * * * *

Back at Erica's house, she was getting her mind together and ready for what her dad was going to say to her. She decided to get her some chamomile tea to calm her nerves. While in her kitchen preparing the tea her dad walked in to have conversation.

"So how are you feeling, my child?"

"I'm good Dad. Just getting some tea so I can go to sleep."

"Well I'm just gone say don't let this situation hinder your mind. I already told you this was gone be a crazy path you chose but I don't want it to break you down mentally."

"Thanks Dad. You know I was waiting for an I told you so."

"You know that's not my style my child, I'm not here to teach you not scold you."

"I am definitely hearing you out each step of the way."

"I hope so because this should be a wakeup call for you. I mean a dead body on your door step? That should tell you a lot."

"Damn, Dad! You didn't have to say it like that!"

"Look at the reality of it! That should be telling you something. How many times have I told you don't let money curse you? You should be growing. It's only paper."

"Okay, Dad. I hear you," Erica said.

Inside she knew she wasn't quitting and missing out on $5,000 just for 15-20 minutes scenes. She wanted to do more to get money she needed. On the other hand, Bishop Williams knew his daughter was addicted to the money. That's why he was telling her to watch her movements. He felt that he told her enough so he was ready to leave.

"Do you need me to stay, my daughter?" he asked.

"Yes, Dad. That would be nice for you to do," she answered.

* * * * *

Sgt. Moretti couldn't believe it -sixty grand he was putting up in his secret safe. While he was putting it up, his wife came in to see what he was doing. She couldn't believe the sight of all the money he was stuffing away.

"Oh my God! Where did you get all that money from?"

"Fuggit about it. All you have to worry about is we about to relocate soon like we planned. I told you that's what we gone do so get ready."

"Okay, but I didn't want you out there doing anything crazy to make that happen."

"Listen I got to do what I got to do, that damn precinct check is not gone cut it I already discussed that with you."

"Okay but I don't want to get that call you hear me?" his wife said getting emotional.

"Trust and believe you won't. I'm making moves that I need to make," Sgt. Moretti said to his wife while kissing her on the forehead.

"Why do you smell like marijuana?"

"Well I was with the Jamaicans, and that's how I'm getting all this money."

"You didn't do anything else did you?" Maria asked her husband, knowing he likes to fuck other women here and there.

"Nope. The thought never crossed my mind," Sgt. Moretti said lying to his wife knowing he just got the best blowjob he ever received in his lifetime.

"I bet you did. You fucking liar!" Maria yelled.

"Hey don't start with me right now Maria! Just know I'm taking care of business."

"Well if you didn't do anything let me smell ya dick, you fucking bastard!"

"Go head and while you're down there you can entertain him with your mouth!"

Maria got down on her knees and sniffed her husband's private parts. She didn't smell anything unusual. Sgt. Moretti was glad he didn't stick his dick in Hot Tottie because he would have been caught red handed. After she was done, she started to entertain her husband's dick.

* * * * *

Chase Money and the Gwap Gang was smoking on some Kush while enjoying the video they made with Tanya and her friends.

"Yo look at Banks smacking the jawn's ass and then putting her titties in his mouth. That nigga is a cold freak boy!" Chase said while laughing so hard he had to hold his stomach.

"Yo hold up, you was in the background for like five minutes, brought out some bottles, then you just disappeared."

"Yo Banks, you right that nigga did just disappear," Paperboi said co-signing with what Banks said about Chase Money.

"Yo I went upstairs with the jawn Tanya. She sucked the shit out my dick y'all. I'm just glad that y'all enjoyed yaselves we got to get ready for these two shows now," Chase said prepping everybody.

After he was done speaking his phone started to ring.

"Yo this King I wonder what he want. Yo King, what's up big homie?"

"I want you to die you disloyal nigga!"

"Yo first of all King what you talking about disloyal? I would never cross you," Chase said getting offended by the words he was hearing coming from King.

"Well word on the street that you robbing me so you have to pay with your life."

"Yo King my squad ain't rob you. Who told you that?"

"Don't worry about who told me just know that you have to watch your back my shottas are gonna light your ass on fire you hear me."

Before Chase could get anything else out King hung up in his ear.

"Yo I know y'all was listening on the convo, we got problems on the streets with King now. So with that being said we got to stay sharp keep our eyes and ear open but at the same time we got to make sure these shows pop off."

Homicide City

Chapter 12

"So what do we have here five bodies in the last couple of days, this is what I want to happen. I want both cases closed," Captain Morello said as he spoke to Detective Patterson and Detective Richmond.

"Also I'm splitting the cases but I need you to huddle and work together and help each other out. Patterson, my man, you the dead Jamaicans case, Richmond you the xxx murder case. But like I said if you two could help each other than that's fine with me as long as we put full closure on these cases. Now did anything surface with this home invasion Patterson?"

"I think it's a cop that did it and that's just my opinion and I say that because it's too clean for a regular."

"Maybe you're right. Do you have any facts to go with your opinion?"

"Captain like I said before when the shit hits the fan, I'm gone be there to say I told you so."

Captain Morello just ignored him and went onto Detective's Richmond's case.

"Now Detective Richmond tell me about any progress you have made with the case so far."

"So far, I got two leads out of the girl sir, one is the girl's baby father he has been calling her but she doesn't know where he is, and second she suspects that one of her favorite customers could be a potential stalker and could have killed the victim through a jealous rage."

"Good. I'm glad to see somebody is already starting to make progress even though I just handed this case to her," Captain Morello said being sarcastic towards Detective Patterson. "Let me ask you this Richmond, what about the father? Don't rule him out. I know he's a bishop but you know them type of people always have a dark side to hide."

"Umm not really ruled out Captain but we keeping a good eye out on him, as a matter of fact me and Patterson gone go by and talk to him to see what we could get out of him."

"Good make sure y'all make that priority."

"All right Captain now let me ask you this what if I don't solve this case with these four dead Jamaicans?"

"Somebody did it damnit, so get me some results," Captain Morello said while they got up and left his office.

"Aren't you lucky? You don't have to get down and dirty on your case. You got suspects to follow up with me I got a needle in a haystack," Detective Patterson said to his partner while they walked out the office.

"Well, not really, cause I got to find out who did this just as well as you do with those four bodies."

"Well you only got one body, I have four and remember King is not folding."

"Well just like Capt said we can help each other so if I think of anything to help you with that's what I'm gone do. We're partners. That's what partners do. But it's time to roll with me for now and head over to Bishop Williams Ministries."

* * * * *

Detective Patterson and Richmond arrived at Bishop Williams Ministries only to find him waiting at the front door.

"Welcome! I felt you guys were on your way so I waited at the front."

These words made Patterson and Richmond look at each other for a quick second.

"Well let's get this over with. I have a couple coming to see me," Bishop Williams said as they followed him to his office.

They walked in his office and sat down and got straight to the point of the matter of why they were there.

"Okay, Bishop Williams. Last night we, didn't implicate that you could be a potential suspect but we do have to consider that you actually could be one. You have every reason to murder in the name of your daughter since I know you don't like the profession she chose, so this is one way to make her stop, but let me say it's one crazy way," Detective Richmond said turning the heat on Bishop Williams.

Her statement made Bishop chuckle before he started to answer her interrogation.

"Now let me just state for the record, I don't have to kill nobody for my daughter to quit porn. She chose that path and I simply told her that getting deeper into that type of business would only bring more grief to her even if she is making a lot of money. Also I'm a millionaire helping people spiritually so why would I put myself in that type of position to have that taken away?"

"That's why we are here to make sure of that," Patterson added to the conversation.

"Well you don't have to implicate me, detective. What you need to do is pay attention to your personal problems. I can look at you right now and see you are having woman problems."

Detective Patterson just stared at him with the blankest look he has ever given a human being.

"How do you know that? What are you psychic or something?"

"Yeah something like that, now onto your partner over here I feel you have a personal issue too and it's affecting your work ethic. Let me just tell you your family member will be okay the situation is only temporary."

"Wow sir you really have a gift. It's my mom she has cancer and you're telling me she will be okay."

"Yes. I get the feeling from you that she is a strong woman and she will be okay."

"Thank you for bringing closure. You made me feel better about the situation Bishop."

"No problem, detective. This is what I do. I'm no killer. I help too many people to go around killing people."

"Well, we are sorry for thinking you would be a suspect."

"No need to apologize you guys were just doing your job and I respect that, but let me give the each of you one of my books. Here's a book for you sir, it's called *Controlling and Understanding Manhood*, and for you ma'am here's a book for you it's called *How to Deal With Reality*. Both books will help you daily.

'Thanks, sir, "Detective Patterson and Richmond said respectively as they grabbed their books and got ready to leave.

"And if there anything else I can do to help, give me a call," Bishop Williams said as he passed them both his cards.

"Thanks Bishop", they both said in unison as they walked out of his office and went on to handle other business.

* * * * *

Erica was chilling at her crib when she received a call from Brian the porn producer.

"I was just about to call you Brian. What's up with you?"

"I was just calling to see if you were ready to film another scene for my next movie. It's called Cum Snatchers and you do it all in this scene anal, oral, and vaginal."

"Now how much am I receiving for this one?"

"Oh I already told you $5,000 a scene. You're my new protégé."

"Okay Brian I'm down but let me ask you did you hear about Mandingo?"

"No. What's up with my main man?"

"He's dead."

"Huh? What are you talking about, dead?"

"He got murdered in front of my house."

"Are you serious? Who the hell would do such a thing?"

"I don't know but I'm assuming that we will find out."

"Well hopefully we will get some closure on that he was definitely a money maker over her at Triple X Productions. Damn. I will surely miss him, but umm let me tell you more about your next scene partner his name is Mr. Hard."

"Okay now why does he call his self Mr. Hard?" Erica asked while laughing at the name.

"I'm not the one to get into all the names and all that. That's for you to ask him."

"Well okay, now what's up with the anal action? Do I really have to go through with that?"

"What's up? You're not feeling the anal?"

"No. Not really. But listen, don't y'all have something that's gone help me handle that if I do, like those anal beads to loosen me up back there?"

"Of course I will give you some to open it up so you won't feel that much pain."

"Okay with that being heard I'm all the way down, but hold on somebody on my other line."

Erica clicked over only to hear nothing as she yelled into the phone and told the person to stop playing on her phone, and then she clicked back over.

"Okay I'm back. Now like I said, Brian, I'm down. Just get what I need and I'm there," Erica said while her phone line beeped again.

"Hold on once again, Brian," she said as she clicked over.

"What's up, Chase?" Erica said as she answered her other line.

"Yo I just wanted to see if you still down for the video/show we got at your spot?"

"Hell yeah, Chase! I'm gone be working so I will definitely be there."

"Are you gone come pass our show tonight?"

"You know what matter of fact I'm gone see what a couple of my girlfriends gone do after work what time you performing."

"We should be performing at 12am. Is that too early for you?"

"As a matter of fact, you know I don't leave the club until after 2 a.m. so it is too early."

"Well, it's cool. Don't worry I will see you at the jawn we have at your spot."

"All right, Chase. See you then."

"All right Erica. I will holla later."

Erica clicked back over with Brian still holding on.

"My fault Brian that was my peoples, but yeah have what I need and it's all good."

"Cool just make it here when you can and I will let Mr. Hard know."

"All right Brian. Let me get myself together and I will be there," Erica said hanging up.

After hanging up she rolled up some Kush then proceeded to get to smoking. She took a couple of puffs then she thought about calling Detective Richmond and leaving her a message about the progress on the suspects she gave her. Detective Richmond didn't answer so she left a message and left her phone number so she could give her a call back.

* * * * *

Detective Patterson and Richmond walked back into the precinct to get everything in order and that's when Detective Richmond received the message from Erica.

"I got to get this phone checked out I didn't even receive the..." Erica said while checking the message.

"Aye partner guess what? That was Bishop's daughter calling me 'bout the two suspects she gave me."

"Good, so give her a call back."

Detective Richmond followed her partner's words stepped to the side and made the call.

"Hello?" Erica said as she answered the phone on the other end.

"Yes. This is Detective Richmond I'm returning your call. Is everything okay?"

"Yes everything is fine I wanted to follow up with you to see if anything worked out with those leads I gave you."

"First off, let me thank you for calling and giving me those leads, but as of right now no but we are working on them believe me when I tell you, but Erica I'm gone call you back to get more info on the two leads."

"Okay thanks detective I really appreciate it," Erica said before she hung up.

"Everything is in working process partner, I just need her to give more info that's all,"

"Cool I'm gone meditate on this book for a minute."

"Yeah you need to do that," Detective Richmond said while laughing and walking away at the same time.

"Ha, Ha," Patterson said as he started to open the book up and read.

As soon as he was about to get to the beginning Richmond walked up with coffee and a donut for her and her partner.

"Thanks partner. Let me ask you a quick question though. Do you think that this man can really help us?"

"Yes I truly do. You have to have more faith partner."

"Yeah I know, but on to the next thing I'm ready to crack this case I'm holding on to but before I do I know something's bout to happen on them streets to where it's gone help me."

"Well hopefully it does cause partner let me tell you, you need a miracle right now."

* * * * *

"Yo are y'all ready for tonight?" Chase Money asked his squad getting them hyped up for the show, "Yo I feel like we gone kill em' tonight but we got to be on the lookout for them nut ass Jamaicans. I don't know what came over King, but I ain't worried about them whatever goes down we gone handle our business. We bout to make a transition anyway, we got to be more aggressive with this rap shit, and takeover the whole city."

"Yeah so what's up this King business he putting us on a drought, Chase?" Paperboi asked.

"Yeah. I know he slowing some things up with this bullshit but once the truth come to the light on the situation then everything will be good cause we all know we ain't hit his houses."

"Well the truth better hurry up cause they slowing up our process of getting our extras that we worked so hard on building up."

"Yeah I feel you on that Paperboi," Banks said getting into the conversation.

"Well like I said Paperboi that's not our main focus no more cause if it's being shut down then it's being shut down for a reason."

"Okay cool I feel you Chase, I see what your saying don't even pay attention to the negative when we can put our energy where it really need to be and that's with that rap shit."

"Exactly. Now you see where I'm going with it. We don't need the bullshit while we building. We just need to stay focus. Are y'all following me?" Chase asked speaking to everybody in the room.

Everybody in the room announced that they were following Chase and understanding him at the same time showing why he was their leader.

"And while we building let's take our minds off Earth for a minute," Scrilla said referring to the Kush.

"Yeah Scrilla, that's what I'm talking about," Banks said while passing him two Dutches to roll up.

"Yeah why we smoke we gone talk about how we gone put the show together and what order we gone do the tracks," Chase said.

* * * * *

Meanwhile, King was holding on to one of the Gwap Gang's flyers for the show tonight waiting for his shottas to arrive. All five of them arrived in orderly fashion as King was rolling a spliff of his finest Kush. He sparked it and began to talk to his brethren.

"My warriors, I'm here to command you to get rid of these pussy clot traitors. Their name is the Gwap Gang, ya hear me now," King said pointing out them on the flyer, "They're the ones who hit me houses and they got to pay, but not by money I want them to pay with their lives, you steal from the King you pay with your life. Me have to put word out that not to fuck with the King."

One of King's men asked to smoke with him and King passed him the nicely rolled spliff to him.

"Here brethren me have plenty rolled up brethren," King said as he picked up another one and lit it up. He blew out the smoke and began to speak again.

"Also we got to keep an eye on that pussy clot Moretti, I tink he's behind some of this madness, but don't worry about him right now let the focus be on The Gwap Gang, then we can focus on Moretti."

* * * * *

"Okay action," Brian the producer said on the set to Mr. Hard as he lubed up his hard penis to insert into Erica's anus.

He also poured some lube onto her ass as it dripped along side of her cheeks onto her pussy as she bent over. Erica was turned on by the feeling of the lube running down her ass onto her pussy. That's when Mr. Hard started to insert his penis into her ass. Erica tensed up and tightened her cheeks at first and it a caused a burning sensation. Then she loosened her muscles and took his entire penis as she moaned like never before. She took it for a good seven minutes and then Brian stopped the scene by yelling out cut.

"Okay cut scene. Over! Now, it's time for the vaginal and cum scene," Brian directed.

That's when Erica got on her back and put her legs in the air as Mr. Hard walked over and inserted his nine inches inside her and had her moaning his name throughout the scene. After ten minutes of hard fucking, he pulled out and squirted on her face as this completed Erica's second scene as a porn star.

"Wow that was great, Mr. Hard! We should do some more scenes together. I enjoyed every bit of that," Erica said while wiping the sperm off her face.

"Yeah I definitely could use you Erica! I'm starting my own company. This was my last scene with Triple X. I feel like it's time for me to move on and become a boss like Brian. If you down just holla at me."

"Well I didn't sign no contract with Brian so I'm entitled to do both."

"Yeah that's right so whenever you ready here's my card. Now get all the money on the side you can. You definitely don't want Brian being the only one making money off of you giving you table scraps."

"What you mean by that? I get $5,000 a scene and that's good for me at the moment."

"And while he gives you five grand, he is making a hundred grand each movie he puts out so it wouldn't be a bad idea for you to double ya money up on the side. That's what Mandingo was doing, God bless his soul, and that's what I was doing."

"Yeah ain't that sad about what happened to Mandingo?"

"Yeah it is but that's why I'm out. I got enough dough saved up and I'm making that transition to becoming a boss."

"Well Mr. Hard. I got your card, now hopefully everything works out for you and we gone see if we gone connect in the future."

Chapter 13

Chase Money and the Gwap Gang had the motorcycle club jumping to their single "Gwapped Up." Chase Money had the mic in the crowd for crowd participation as he repeated the hook.

"U know I'm Gwapped Up! U know I'm Gwapped Up! Catch me in ya hood you can tell that I'm Gwapped Up".

Everybody in the crowd knew every single word and went along with the whole Gwap Gang until the song ended.

"Listen up everybody we are the new movement to move with. Take a look at the shirts GwapGang.com download the EP. We are moving nobody fucking with us right now if you don't believe me go download the EP, the proof is in the pudding. I hope y'all enjoyed the show, y'all got the flyers for tomorrows show we gone be at club onyx shutting it down just like we did this one plus we gone be filming the for our single "We Gwapped Up."

After Chase was finished, the rest of the gang knew it was time to mingle with some females and fall back. So they went to the bar ordered a couple bottles of Grey Goose, found a spot to post up and that's when some of their fans walked up on them.

"Oh my God! We loving the song, Chase Money!"

"That's what's up, now what's ya name sweetheart?"

"My name is Shannon and these are my BFF's Jocelyn, Christine, Tia, and Nyjah," Shannon said playing host and being the vocal one out of the crew.

'Well over here we got my squad Banks, Paperboi, Scrilla, and Stacks."

It always has to be one out of the female bunch that always asked dumb questions and it was one of Chase's pet peeves.

"So why do y'all call yourselves the Gwap Gang?" Shannon asked.

"Cause we about that Gwap, Gwap is a slang word for money," Chase said shaking his head.

"Cool now are y'all sharing that goose? I'm trying to get loose too," Nyjah asked.

"Of course we are," Banks answered as he grabbed a bottle and cuffed Nyjah up by swinging his arm around her waist.

"Okay you claiming me already, huh?" Nyjah asked.

"Yeah you can say that."

The rest of the squad knew what time it was therefore Scrilla hopped on Christine, Paperboi gripped up Jocelyn, and Stacks hollered at Tia. Everything was flowing greatly they knew it was only a matter of a couple of sips off the goose that they would be able to take them back to the crib. Chase Money phone started to ring so he stepped off into the bathroom so he could here whoever was calling.

"Yo what's up? Who this?" Chase said while answering his phone talking over the loud music.

"You're a dead man walking," the voice on the other end told him.

"Oh Yeah? Fuck you, whoever you are. I'm getting money and you just a hater!" he yelled through the receiver and then hung up.

He stepped out the bathroom and went back to mingling with his squad along with Shannon and her squad. He waited till the girls got tipsy after they popped their bottles to give the announcement that the after party was gone be at their crib.

"Y'all ready to leave with us and hop over to the Gwap Gang Mansion?" Chase asked Shannon and her crew.

"Hell yeah we rolling out with the Gwap Gang!" Shannon said to her squad as they started to laugh from being intoxicated.

"Cool cause we out right now," Chase said as they got their belongings and walked out towards the exit.

When they reached outside a couple of cops we seen posted up monitoring the traffic just in case something went down from all the people coming in for the afterhours. Now as Chase and the Gang stepped out they knew they had to get their burners they stashed so they dipped off real quick and collected them where they left them. Now where they parked under the el train was crowded with fans walking pass yelling out how much they loved them as they had to take a couple of flicks with the fans. Then they decided to roll out after as Chase hopped in his Grand Marquis along with Shannon in the passenger seat and Paperboi and Jocelyn hopped in the back. Banks, Scrilla and Stacks hopped in Banks Lesabre and they jawns had to lap up in the back with them as Banks told Nyjah to hop in the front with him, once they had everybody assembled they pulled off and went straight on 60th and Market.

"I'm hungry we should go to McDonald's on 52nd Street," Shannon suggested before they made it back to the crib.

"Okay cool," Chase said as he pulled out his cell to hit up Banks and tell him that was their destination before the crib.

"Yo Banks. We going to McDonald's on 52nd Street."

"Cool," Banks said as he hung up.

As they passed 56th and Market Banks pulled out his cell and hit up Chase on his.

"Yo somebody is following me Chase, and I think I seen dreads but I ain't sure you know my vision a little off from the goose."

"Oh shit! Y'all be easy. That might be King's men, but we still gone go to McDonalds, if they make a move we dumping on them plain and simple."

As they made it to 52nd and Market they made a right onto 52nd St, then drove up till they got to Chestnut and stopped at a red light. While at the red light Banks hit up Chase again.

"Yo ain't nobody behind us no more so we should be straight for now, but I still say we need to play this one close while we out like this."

"Most definitely now let's pull up in this McDonald's and get something to eat. I'm starving my nigga," Chase said as he pulled up to the drive thru and ordered the whole car some food.

As he was done ordering and got their food he pulled to side and parked and waited for Banks to order and get their food. When Banks was done he pulled up next to Chase and hopped out to holla at him.

"Yo whoever was behind me ain't nowhere in sight now? I don't know if them niggas made a turn off somewhere or what but let's just make it back to the crib now."

"Yeah you right, Banks. Ain't no need to get into anything that will blow our spot up plus you got the patrol car sitting right here. What niggas in their right mind would do some shit like that?"

While Banks and Chase were having their conversation that's when King's men pulled up at the light on Chestnut St. and 52nd staring right across from the McDonald's.

"Dere they go right there!" the driver pointed out as they tried to creep up on them. But it was too late Chase and them were already expecting them when they pulled up and started dumping on Chase and Banks as everybody ducked from the shots. Glass was flying everywhere, as Shannon and her friends were screaming from all the gunshots. Chase and Banks got up after the shots were done and told everybody on the squad to get out and make sure everybody wasn't hit and to dump their hammers. The squad car jumped right on the Jamaicans as they tried to get away after spraying up the McDonald's parking lot by making a right onto 51st St. After Chase and the squad dumped their hammers, they wanted to get away from the scene so they made a quick right onto 51st, but as soon as they were about to make the right to get away to squad cars were coming up 51st St. and pulled them over.

"Get the fuck out of the car!" the cops yelled as they drew their guns and pulled everybody out the cars.

When the cops pulled everybody out Chase peeped how he saw a car flipped over at the corner of 51st and Walnut. The cops that pulled them over were busy searching their cars to see if they had any guns, but Chase and the rest of the squad made the right move by dumping their guns. By the time the cops were done searching that's when an ambulance was pulling up to the scene where the Jamaicans car flipped over, then two more squad cars pulled up on the scene where the Gwap Gang was pulled over at.

"Look I know the car is clean. Y'all still going in for questioning for this shootout."

"Damn man. We get shot at and we got to go in for questioning? That's fucked up!" Chase said.

"Watch ya dam mouth and shut up and get in the car," the cop told Chase as they rounded up the rest of the Gwap Gang.

"Look y'all lovely ladies can either wait here or go y'all separate ways," one cop said to Shannon and her squad.

Shannon decided that it would be best if they stayed as she walked over to the squad car Chase was in and got his keys, then Nyjah followed suit and got Bank's keys.

"Look y'all mine as well follow us to the station," Chase said to Shannon.

Shannon and Nyjah decided that they were gone drive to the precinct with them and wait there. When they pulled up to the precinct and led everybody to the holding cell one officer decided to call Detective Patterson.

"Hello. This is Detective Patterson."

"Yeah Officer Brown here. I think you should make it over to the precinct. It was a shootout that occurred that should help your case."

"Okay good work! I'm on my way in," Detective Patterson said before he hung up.

* * * * *

Detective Richmond was outside Club Onyx waiting for Erica to call her. As soon as she dozed off a little that's when she received the call from her.

"Detective this is Erica, I'm in the bathroom. Can you hear me?"

"Yes I can hear you fine. Now what's the problem?"

"Okay good there's no problem. I just wanted you to know that the man is standing at the front door as we speak."

"Okay. Give me a quick description."

"He's a tall diesel dark-skinned man and he has on a Gucci outfit on."

"Okay thanks. I'm on it, Erica," Detective Richmond said as she hopped out her car and proceeded to walk inside.

As she walked to the front, the bouncer patted her down and made her pay to get in like she was a regular customer. He told her she couldn't get in with her gun not knowing she was a cop so she showed of her shiny badge and then he let her in. As she stepped in she saw Omar standing there with a dancer cuffing her ass and whispering something in her ear. Detective Richmond walked up on him and tapped him on the shoulder disrupting the conversation Omar was having with the young lady.

"Mr.? May I have a couple of words with you?"

As she was done Omar turned around with a clueless look on his face from not knowing what was going on.

"What you stalking me now Natasha?" Omar said as he turned around and recognized her before she recognized him.

"Oh my God! Omar, what's up? I'm here picking up my cousin," Detective Richmond said changing up her story.

"For real who's your cousin?"

"Her name is Erica, do you know her?"

"Oh that's my favorite stripper in here! She will tell you I'm her #1 fan."

The word he just uttered would have been perfect for a motive but Detective Richmond knew this wasn't the man she was looking for. She pulled out her cell phone and called Erica back and told her to meet her in the front lobby. Erica walked up in a matter of minutes greeting Omar in the process.

"Hey Omar!"

"What's up Silk-E? I didn't know you had a cousin in the precinct."

"Yeah this is my cousin," Erica said not knowing what was going on.

"Cool I will holla at you later though. I'm about to head back in," Omar said gripping the young girl and taking her back into the club.

"Girl what was that about?" Erica asked as they walked out.

"Erica, let me just put it to you like this Omar is not your guy because I was fucking him the night in question."

"Wow so how was the dick, detective? I know it was good that man has a big one."

"Oh it was great! He knows how to please the woman."

173

As soon as she was about to get into detail on their night her phone started ringing and it was her partner.

"What's up Patterson?"

"Where you at, Richmond? I need you to meet me at the station ASAP."

"Okay cool. Say no more. I'm on my way."

"Look Erica, I'm needed over at the station. If you come across anything else, just call me."

"Okay detective. I will do that," Erica said as they parted ways.

As soon as Erica stepped in the car her phone started ringing. To the left, to the left blasted out her phone, as she knew who was calling as she answered.

"Hey Dawud, how have you been?" Erica said.

"I'm good, I was calling to tell you I have been out in AC gambling for the last couple of days, and when I get back I'm gone toss you a couple of hundred for DJ."

"Okay cool, Dawud. I will talk to you when you get back."

"Damn you got to get off the phone with me that fast? You must got a another nigga around."

"Listen Dawud. I don't have anyone around me for one. Second I just got off work and I'm tired so just call me when you get back to Philly okay?"

"All right talk to you later," Dawud said as he hung up.

"Damn. That cancels him out too," Erica said as she started her car up.

Homicide City

Chapter 14

Detective Richmond arrived at the precinct in twenty minutes flat. She parked diligently and precise only to hop out and fast walk it into the precinct, and when she walked in her she went straight to the interrogation room where she peeked in and saw her partner so she stepped in.

"Hey partner. Say hello to Chase Money, Chase Money say hello to my partner," Detective Patterson said as she walked in.

"Hey partner!" Chase Money said being sarcastic.

"So this is Chase Money! What brings you here, Chase?" Detective Richmond asked.

"Man. I don't even want to be here."

"Well let me ask you in a different way. What did you do to make it into this room?"

"I didn't do nothing. Me and my squad was chilling in the parking lot at McDonald's on 52nd St. and these wild niggas started blasting on us."

"I think you're leaving something out, Chase, cause why would the Jamaicans just shoot at you for fun? We want to know why you were a target."

"Well look at me! Read the shirt. We the Gwap Gang. We get money and niggas hate us."

"Okay I understand that you're the quote on quote Gwap Gang and y'all make music you have your own website but it's no coincidence that these men are Jamaican and they are targeting you guys."

"What do you mean coincidence? I don't understand what you're saying."

"Well I will help you understand," Detective Patterson said, "Okay. Now the coincidence is that they are Jamaican, and King... I know you know King, he sent these men to kill you because you did something to King and his men. Now tell me what I need to know."

"Wow detective that's a good scenario! You know you should write a book that story you just put together can be a best seller!"

"And you should be a fucking comedian!" Patterson shot back at Chase.

"Now you know what the fuck I'm talking about Chase! Let's not play games here."

Chase just gave him a stare down for a minute or so without saying anything.

"Listen don't try and stall, but take ya time cause we are not fools here them Jamaicans were after you for a reason so break it down for me."

"Okay man let me break it down. I received a call from King and he called me talking bout I was robbing his houses."

"Wait a minute you said he said houses? It was only one on paper that was robbed."

"Man. He told me houses."

"Now let me tell you. It was four dead bodies involved in the one house that I know of now can you tell me about that."

"Hell no cause me and my squad didn't rob no houses, and we damn sure don't know about no bodies."

"Oh shit! The more he talks, the more that this shit is starting to make sense to me Richmond!" Detective Patterson said getting excited.

"Aye man don't try and look at me as no snitch! I'm just letting you know how I was involved. Yeah I did a little dirt on the streets but take a look my shirt, I'm done with that route."

"I believe you but why would you get that call? Who told King that it was you unless he just pulled your name out of hat?"

"I don't know all I know is I'm out and not into that shit no more. That shit is getting to deep for me."

"Yeah I believe you and I hope everything works out for you with the music business so you won't have to step back into the streets."

"Thanks man. So does that mean me and my squad are free to go now?"

"Yeah, y'all are free to go," Patterson said as he stepped out and told Officer Johnson that the Gwap Gang was free to go.

"So why did you just let him go like that, partner?" Richmond asked.

"Because Richmond I figured it all out," Detective Patterson said while grabbing his keys.

"So where you off to now?" Detective Richmond said at the site of her partner grabbing his keys.

"Oh. I'm going to visit a special someone."

* * * * *

"Ooh Frank, fuck me Frank. Ooh yeah fuck me Frank!" Karen yelled as Frank went in and out of her pussy like a jackhammer.

Sgt. Moretti was showing off for the camera he had setup but Karen didn't know it.

"Yeah take this dick, Karen!" Moretti said while he went in and out of her.

He even cocked her legs in the air and pointed in the camera showboating for the recording and pumped in and out faster as he was about to cum. Sgt. Moretti let out a large grunt. It was so intense when he released himself.

"Oh my God! That felt so good, Frank! You're nothing like my husband!"

"Yeah. Tony is too old to fuck you like this. Eating all that pasta is slowing him down," Sgt. Moretti bragged at the fact that he was fucking the boss's wife.

"How do you think he would feel if he knew you were fucking me, Frank?"

"I mean it's his own fault Karen. Did you even mention Viagra to the man?" Sgt. Moretti asked laughing.

"You are so funny, but yes I did. All he is worried about now a days is more money. He doesn't give two shits about me half the time."

"We'll see what comes of that when that happens," Sgt. Moretti said with a grin on his face. As he was smiling he caught an epiphany about how Detective Patterson always was getting to fuck other men's wives.

His phone started to ring.

"Look speaking of the devil here we are fucking and talking about him, then he calls. Don't even breathe while I'm on the phone with him. Hey Tony what can I do for you boss?"

"Where you been at, Frank? I've been trying to reach you for like a week now."

"Oh I know I should've told you Tony, but I rented a car and I'm on vacation out Jersey."

"Well get your ass back to Philly we have some unfinished business to take care of!"

"Well can it wait till I get back Tony cause I'm tied up here."

"You know I don't talk over phones. Now get your ass back to Philly."

"Damn, Tony! You're sending for me!"

"Yes, I'm sending for you. It's time for us to have a sit down."

"Okay. I'm on my way."

"So what does he want, Frank?" Karen asked.

"He wants to have a sit down with me and to tell you the truth I don't like the sound of it at all. I hope I don't have to end up killing your husband, Karen."

"I mean you make it easier on me Frank. What I need with a man that has a limp dick? If you do, I still get the house and half of the money."

"Wow, but I didn't mean it that way. I have a lot of respect for Tony. He's taught me a lot and I know I went against some things he said but now it comes down to a sit down."

"Well still go and see what the sit down is about you owe him that much respect Frank."

"You know what Karen? You're right. That's what I'm gonna do."

* * * * *

The only Jamaican that survived the car crash had a cousin come visit him at the University of Penn Hospital where he was at after the injuries he sustained in the crash.

The cousin was coming to get info on Chase Money and the Gwap Gang, and when he came he brought flowers and his girlfriend so it could seem like the visit was meaningful. His cousin also knew that he was under custody of the police since the other three died in the crash, and they would be at the door watching every visitor that came in. As they made it in the hospital, the cousin and his girlfriend went through the proper id check and signing the visitor list and went to the designated room where his cousin was. When they made it to the room, the officer patted them down and checked their ids before they were allowed to go in, and since everything checked out with the front desk they were granted access. When they went in they greeted each other and the man gave his cousin all the info King told him on the Gwap Gang.

* * * * *

Erica was in her usual mode smoking some Kush while she was watching the news, and that's when the news showed what happened with the Jamaicans as they mentioned the Gwap Gang involvement.

"I hope Chase and them are okay," she said as she was watching the news. She then decided to call Chase to get the scoop to see if he was okay.

"Yo Chase what's up? Are you guys okay? I just heard about what happened."

"Yeah we cool, you know we don't let the haters get in the way of progress. We still got our show at your club and we still shooting the video."

"Well that's why I was calling, to make sure that was still going down."

"Oh hell yeah! Like I said, we don't pay attention to the negative that niggas is throwing our way. We already know we got to keep it moving."

"That's what's up Chase," Erica said as her other line clicked.

"That's my other line Chase, I will hit you up later. Hello?" Erica said answering her other line.

"Erica could you come to the office and bring your detective friend with you? Mr. Hard and Brian are arguing intensely and I think something's bout to happen."

"Well why would I bring her for only an argument? That would be wasting her time."

"Well let me just say I was eavesdropping and you should bring her up here."

"Okay Candice. I hope I'm not wasting her time," Erica said as she hung up and called Detective Richmond and told her to meet her at the Triple X studio office.

* * * * *

Back at the Triple X offices Brian and Mr. Hard were knee deep in a heated discussion based on Mr. Hard leaving.

"So you mad Brian cause I learned the business and I want to leave your company and start my own?"

"It's the fact that you used me."

"How did I use you and I made you millions in the process all I got was table scraps?"

"So now you did it cause you were ungrateful of the money I was bringing you?"

"No I'm not ungrateful Brian. It's the fact that you want people to stay up under you so you can make all the money, but like I said earlier that's over with. I'm leaving."

"But with you leaving I know you're going to try and take Erica away from me!"

"I'm not trying to take her away from you Brian, but she has already agreed to be in my first movie!"

"So you did that without approaching me how are you making business moves with my people without consulting me?"

"Well I just told you now since you speculating that I'm trying to take her away from you even though I'm not!"

Erica and Detective Richmond entered the building and were on their way up to the offices while Brian and Mr. Hard were still arguing.

"Okay so all this meeting is about you coming up here and dissolving our relationship, huh?"

"Yeah basically. That's what this meeting was all about me telling you I'm leaving and starting my own company, it's only business and you're taking it personal,"

"Well Mr. Hard you won't be called Mr. Hard when I get done with you today," Brian said pulling out a razor that resembles a box cutter to slice Mr. Hard up.

"Oh so you're the mothafucker that killed Mandingo! It all makes sense now! He wanted to leave and you killed him; I want to leave and you're trying to kill me. Well let me tell you I ain't going out like Mandingo!"

"We'll see about that!" Brian said as he took a swipe at Mr. Hard's cheek, slicing him to the white meat.

After his first swipe Detective Richmond stormed into the room with her gun drawn and told Brian to drop the razor.

"Now why should I drop it officer when this man is trying to attack me? I was man enough to take it away and use it to my defense!"

"No he's lying and I have proof," Brian's assistant said coming into the room amongst all the commotion.

"Now what evidence do you have? You don't know shit, bitch!"

Candice pulled out the recorder and played the small tape with Brian speaking on it saying if Mr. Hard leaves him he will end up like Mandingo. After hearing the tape Brian was outraged.

"You fucking whore!" He said as he lunged at her with the razor.

As quick as he lunged at her Detective Richmond shot him in his shoulder and stopped him in his tracks.

"You're under arrest, Brian, for the murder of Mandingo. You have the right to remain silent," Detective Richmond said getting into the arresting Miranda.

"I'm glad this is over," Erica said as she went over to Mr. Hard to see if he was okay.

"Thanks Erica. I'm okay. I just need a few stitches. That's all."

* * * * *

"So you mean to tell me ya husband put in a two week resignation a week ago?"

"Yes Detective Patterson. He said he was done with being a cop."

Detective Patterson couldn't believe what he was hearing. He always had it in the back of his mind that Sgt. Moretti was the cause of the streets being in a frenzy.

"So where is he at now? His car is parked in the driveway."

"I told you I don't know. He left a week ago without telling me."

"He left a week ago and he didn't tell you where he was going? That's very hard to believe Mrs. Moretti."

"Well I don't know. What else can I tell you detective?"

"Okay here's my card. Call me if he shows his face any time soon."

Chapter 15

Sgt. Moretti walked into Tony Moretti's café not knowing what he was walking into. This was one feeling he never felt since this was his first time being sent for.

"Hey Tony," Frank Moretti said as he greeted his boss with a kiss on his cheek.

As he was finished greeting Tony, Johnny Capers and Joey Five Fingers walked out of the back of the café.

"Hey what's up Frank?" they both greeted him nonchalantly.

That's when Frank felt something strange in the air, but he held his composure.

"Sit down Frank we have to talk serious business," Tony said as Frank followed his orders.

"So what's up, Tony? What was so important that I had to be sent for?"

"Well first off tell me why you're the reason that my deal with King didn't fall through."

"I'm not gone lie Tony, I found a opening and way that I could make money and I'm sorry for being so selfish towards the family, I know now I should have came to you and put family first."

"I don't want to hear your sympathy you have to pay for your mistakes, do I make myself clear?"

Right when Tony was done Johnny Capers walked up behind Frank and wrapped a wire around his throat, and then Joey came around and kicked him in the chest to knock him on his back. The momentum from the kick let Frank free from the wire that Johnny had wrapped around his throat as he quickly got up on his feet elbowed Johnny in the mouth and kicked Joey in the nuts. After putting them in pain, he quickly brandished the nine he came in with and pointed it at Tony.

"So is this what it was supposed to come down to? You have them two kill me! Why couldn't you do it, you coward?"

"Never mind that Frank you hold the power now, so if you want to kill me do it."

"You know what I have too much respect for you to kill you Tony. On the other hand you just showed me you don't have the same respect for me. I'm not gone hold that against you I'm just gone walk out of here and you don't have to see or hear from me again," Frank Moretti said while walking backwards toward the door.

He ended up walking backward until he knew that no one was following him or was gone try anything so he made his getaway smoothly.

"You're gone let him just walk away Tony?" Johnny Capers asked through all the pain he was feeling from the elbow he just took.

"You don't have to worry about him. He's not coming back."

"Okay boss I was just asking."

"But let me ask you this I see a lot of blood leaking out of your mouth. How does it feel?"

"Oh it's very painful. I need to go to the hospital and see a dentist."

"Well everything will be okay you don't have to suffer no more," Tony said as he pulled out a .32 from the back of his pants and put a bullet between Johnny's eyes. Joey Capers stood in shock still holding his nuts from Frank's kick. After taking a quick glimpse at Johnny he looked up and Tony stood over him aiming the .32 at his cranium. All Joey heard was the loud bang as his life was taking away from a single shot to the brain.

"Now I know y'all didn't think you two was getting away with what you did. Y'all fucked up thousands from me!" Tony said at the top of his lungs.

After murdering them he pulled out his cell and called one of his workers Paulie to come and get rid of the bodies.

"Hey Paulie I have a job for you. Get some lime and shovels. You got a burial service to handle."

* * * * *

Everybody clapped for Detective Richmond as she walked into the precinct, showing her respect for her first major collar. She basked in the glory giving out thank yous in the process.

"Good work partner!" Detective Patterson said.

"Yes show my detective praise! She deserves it," Captain Morello said as he clapped along with the rest of the officers.

Detective Patterson turned to look at Captain Morello and gave his boss a nasty stare as he walked into his office.

"Why am I the last to know everything around here?"

"What did I hold back from you Patterson?"

"The fact that your Sgt. put in a 2 weeks resignation when all that crazy shit was going down and you stood back and did nothing."

"It's deeper than what you think it is Patterson."

"Okay so what type of explanation is that coming from the Captain?"

"That's all I'm entitled to let you know right now."

"Capt, I'm not taking that for an answer. I'm sorry you gone have to do better that that!"

"What the hell do you want from me Patterson? I told him he was getting out of control. He crossed a line I told him clearly not to cross. He didn't listen and now he's paying for it."

"Okay Captain I get it it's between you two so I'm gone stay out of it," Detective Patterson said as he left the office.

* * * * *

"Yo let's go y'all! We got to get out so we can promote this show tonight," Chase Money said speaking to the rest of the Gwap Gang.

"Yo while we out do you think that we got to worry about any more of King's men?" Banks asked.

"You know what Banks we gone strap up but from now on fuck da haters as long as we prepared to dump back we good now let's focus on moving forward," Chase Money said speaking like the true leader he was.

"Yeah I feel on that good brother."

"But before we move out I got to stop pass my mom crib to a holla at my baby bro."

Everybody was cool with that long as it didn't interfere with the time they had to put in work with promoting. Everybody got ready grabbed their nines individually, tucked them and was ready to roll out and handle their business.

"We straight, everybody strapped now we out," Chase commanded.

As they walked around Walnut The Gwap Gang ran into Erica and her friend Janine from the club they dance at.

"Yo what's up Erica you ready for tonight?"

"Yeah Chase I can't wait for tonight!"

"Who's ya friend?" Banks asked while grilling her.

"Oh this my friend Janine! Janine this is the Gwap Gang, as you can see on their shirts."

"Oh my god this the squad that came out with that song Gwapped Up! I bought the ringtone," Janine said as she pulled out her cell and showed them proof that she was a fan.

"Yo that's what's up," the whole Gwap Gang agreed as they witnessed a real live fan in person besides their shows that dig their music.

"Just for that you get a slot in the video along with Erica."

"That's what's up! Thank you," Janine said.

"All right we on the move we will see y'all later," Chase said as they walked towards 56th and Walnut.

As they walked away they could hear the excitement coming from Janine as she was calling someone telling them she was gone be in the video. The Gwap Gang walked up on 56 and Walnut and made a left on 56th St. to stop at Chase Mom's crib. When they reached the destination Chase's brother Chance was sitting on the step chilling as usual.

"What's up? I'm rolling with the Gwap Gang today."

"Shut up li'l nigga! We said we were taking you so don't ask any more. Now where's ya t-shirt? You can't go nowhere with us unless you got the Gwap Gang t-shirt on."

"All right Chase let me go throw it on," Chance said as he ran into the house.

Five minutes later he came back out and was ready to roll only to have their mom follow him to the door.

"Aye Chase you sure nothing happens to my son, you hear me? It's bad enough I'm gone let my future chief of police hang with you."

"Mom, chill. Ain't nothing wrong with making music. I'm making money and taking care of myself and my squad."

"Whatever Chase you know what I mean, all that shoot 'em up bang-bang shit could be left out."

"Don't start with that mom. Just be happy I'm not locked up somewhere and not doing nothing."

As soon as Chase was done talking to his mom a car pulled up on 56th and Walnut blasting reggae ready to make a turn onto 56th St. The car made the Gwap Gang get focused and be on alert as they passed by.

"Yo I thought we was gone have to start dumping on somebody real quick," Scrilla said.

The driver of the vehicle that just passed them stopped at 56th and Locust and pulled over and made a quick phone call.

"Hey Knotty Dread they are all outside as you said they would be."

"Cool I'm about to pull up now," Knotty Dread said as he hung up and pulled up on 56th and Walnut in his all black Tahoe.

"Yo Chase I'm gone run in and go to the bathroom to real quick to pee. I will be right back."

"Yo Chance we on a tight schedule c'mon man hurry up!"

Knotty Dread jumped the light and road pass the Gwap Gang, and his shotta popped a couple of shots as he made them scatter and duck seeking cover as he let off. Nobody could get off a shot as they pulled the drive-by and made a left on Locust. Screams could be heard coming from inside Chase Mom's house, as they got louder as she came running to the front door. As she came to the front door she seen her baby boy laid out from taking a shot to the pelvis unable to move.

"Chance can you hear me! Chance can you hear me?" She yelled frantically.

"Yes mom I can hear you. I just feel numb right now," Chance said looking up at his mom.

Chase ran up on the porch holding his arm from a shot he took.

"Chase you hit too! Oh my God both my babies shot! Oh Lord!"

"Listen, Mom snap out of it and call an ambulance! The cops are already on their way. Somebody must have already called them."

"Ayo! Y'all go dump them hammers somewhere," Chase yelled out to his squad.

"Aye li'l' bro! Hold on! Help is on the way for you," Chase said to his little brother as he stood over him.

As soon as the squad cars pulled up they jumped out and ran up on the porch where Chance was laid out.

"Look there's a wounded victim and he lost a lot of blood make sure an ambulance is on the way," Officer Freeman called out to his assisting officer.

"Ambulance is already on the way," the dispatch said over the radio

The rest of the officers started questioning everyone on the scene to get answers on what happened. Then five minutes later the ambulance showed up and got Chance on the truck in an orderly fashion, as Chase mom hopped in along with them. They even told Chase to get on to make sure they could get him medical attention from his gunshot wound. Chance heart rate started to drop from losing so much blood from his gunshot wound. So the Medics started to give him oxygen to get his heart rate up, but it was too late to start any other procedures Chance started to flat line in the back of the ambulance. At the sight of her son dying in back of the ambulance Chase's mom passed out and went into shock from all the screaming and crying.

Back on the block Erica and Janine ran down to see what happened, as they ran up they ran into Banks who just got done being questioned by the cops.

"Yo, what happened?" Erica said being concerned.

"Yo Jamaicans pulled a drive-by on us and Chase and Chance got popped."

"I know who it was. It was the crazy Jamaican boy Knotty."

"Who the fuck is Knotty?" Banks asked.

"Some crazy Jamaican boy that I know. I seen him when he passed my crib before all the shooting occurred."

"Oh okay good looking out now we got a car and a name. But as of now we bout to go to the hospital and see how Chase and Chance is making out, now I don't know if we gone have that show tonight."

* * * * *

Sgt. Moretti pulled up to his house and jumped out his car. His wife came running to the door once she heard him pull up.

"Frank, a detective was looking for you. His name is Detective Patterson. What kind of trouble are you in?" his wife asked at the sight of the blood from him elbowing Johnny earlier.

"Listen. Don't worry about that. Did you get everything I said to get?"

"Yes I packed everything you said to pack."

"Good your gonna take the rental. I GPS'D the destination so you can leave before me and I will be right behind you."

"Okay baby give me a kiss! I love you Frank. Now let me grab one more thing and I will be ready."

"Don't worry baby. I'm gone be right behind you. I have to grab something too."

Frank ran in the house to his little attic closet pulled the string and a duffle bag dropped from the ceiling. He grabbed the bag and was on his way out when he noticed that his wife grabbed everything except the furniture.

"We didn't need it any way the new house is furnished," he stated out loud as he said goodbye to the old house and ran out. As he ran out he saw that his wife was already up a block away, so he hurried up started the car and was out of the driveway in no time.

She stopped at the stop sign at the end of the block so Frank can catch up, and while she sat there she spotted Frank threw the rearview stopping and stalling in the car. Then the unthinkable happened, the car when up in an explosion. She let out the most frantic scream as she got out and ran towards the explosion screaming out his name.

T. Real

Chapter 16

"They took my baby away from me! Why did they have to take my baby? Why lord why!" Chases mother screamed at the funeral.

A few of the men in the family had to grab her before she fell out, and they even had to stop her from jumping into the casket a few times while asking God to take her along with him. Everybody had on their "The good die young", T-shirts with Chance's face on it along with his born date and his ill-fated departure. Chase had to step outside from all the chaos to catch some air as Banks followed him out to make sure he was straight.

"Yo you straight, Chase? I know this is hard for you to take in."

"Yeah I'm straight, Banks. I just had to step out I couldn't take seeing my moms acting like that, her screaming and crying was getting to me a little bit."

"Yeah I feel you my nigga, but you got to be strong for her now even though it's gone be a tough one."

"Yeah I know I got to step up and be strong for her, but as I think more and more about what happened I wonder what God is trying to tell me since my brother was taking away since you know shit happens for a reason."

"That is between you and God, Chase, but let me just tell you this: he must have been needed to guide you as an angel for you to be guided the right way."

"Damn, Banks. That's a good way to look to at the situation my nigga. Good looking out, I needed that my nigga," Chase said as he got the strength to go back and handle the rest of the funeral.

* * * * *

"Aim, fire!" *Pow!* "Aim, fire!" *Pow!* "Aim, fire!" *Pow!* "Aim, fire!" *Pow!* Those last four shots completed the 21-gun salute for Sgt. Moretti. As the shots were going off, each one of them jerked the tears of Maria, his wife, as she held their daughter Michelle in her arms. As they finished, she just stared at the photo of her late husband and wondered how it was going to be becoming a widow and was she strong enough to move on.

"Mommy… Daddy's in heaven right now, right?" Michelle asked in her innocent voice.

"Yes Michelle. Daddy is in heaven, and he's watching over us," Maria replied as they got up and took the flag and walked away.

Captain Morello wanted to talk to Maria but he was stopped in his tracks by a voice that he thought he would never here again in his life.

"Hey Morello good to see you. It's been a long time," Tony Moretti said.

"Yeah it's been a long time, Moretti."

"And it's so sad that we had to meet under such raw circumstances. I mean you could've stopped him but you didn't. He was just like you were stuck in between two worlds you let go and now look. Now why is that Captain when you could've told him what you already know?"

"Look Moretti the past is the past now don't come over to me trying to dig up old shit, and second I don't have to explain nothing to you. I'm just gone leave you with these kind words. This is just the beginning now remember I told you that," Captain Morello said as he walked away to talk to Maria to give her his condolences.

Detectives Patterson and Richmond both paid their respects to Sgt. Moretti's grave then Detective Patterson walked over to Mrs. Moretti as Detective Richmond walked over to her partner's car to wait for him.

"Hello Mrs. Moretti, I'm sorry that we have to meet again under these type of circumstances."

"It's okay Detective, life goes on, right?" Mrs. Moretti said as she started to tear up again but kept her composure as she spoke again, "Listen I'm glad you stopped passed my house before this happened. It shows that you were concerned for my husband and I'm grateful for that, so thank you detective."

"Your welcome and I'm sure you heard this from my Captain but if it's anything you need please don't hesitate to call me you still have my card, right?"

"Yes Detective I still have your card."

"Okay well I'm gone leave now. My partner's waiting. You take it easy Mrs. Moretti,"

Detective Patterson said as he walked away towards his car where his partner was waiting.

"How is she holding up?" Detective Richmond asked.

"She's okay, I guess. To me, it seems she will get through this. From what I see she's a strong woman," Detective Patterson said as they both got into his car.

"So where we off to now?" Detective Richmond asked her partner.

"I was thinking we should get something to eat partner."

"Sounds good to me cause a bitch is hungry," Detective Richmond said as they both laughed.

"I know the perfect place down Old City, it's called The Continental."

"Cool. Let's go", Detective Richmond said as her partner pulled off.

While driving to the destination Detective Richmond brought up something she thought her partner didn't observe.

"Hey partner, did you see Captain Morello talking to the mob boss Moretti?"

"What you think I didn't? Believe me, I see everything."

"Well I only asked cause I thought you didn't see them and I was wondering about what was said in the conversation."

"I was wondering the same thing when I saw them."

After getting something to eat Detective Patterson dropped off his partner and proceeded to go home. On his way there he thought about how he wanted to indulge in some sexual activities. He wanted to call Aneesa just to piss off her husband but he decided not to. He even laughed to himself at the thought of that while he walked to his door to enter his condo. As he walked up he found his door cracked open, he quickly pulled out his gun then slowly crept in his house. As he crept in, he smelled cigarette smoke so he followed the smell into his living and walked in on a silhouette of a person sitting in the dark smoking a cigarette. Patterson turned on the light but not without pointing his gun towards the person that was sitting on his couch, and when he did he couldn't believe who it was. The culprit just sat there still smoking their cigarette like Patterson wasn't there pointing a gun at them. Patterson was the first one that broke silence.

"What the fuck are you doing in my house?"

The man who broke in just took another puff from his cigarette and sat in silence and didn't answer the question. Detective Patterson started to get irritated and his patience was growing thin with the man especially since he was still sitting in silence and to add to that he was smoking in his condo, he didn't let anyone smoke in his condo. He decided to take a different approach with conversation.

"So are you gone even acknowledge my questioning or do I have to put a bullet in you?"

Detective Patterson asked while still pointing the gun at the culprit.

The threat of the gun made the man laugh as he answered.

"Detective no need to send threats. Where do you want me to start?"

"Well let's start off by telling me how did you survive the hit?"

"What hit? You mean to tell me you think that was a hit? C'mon Detective! You surprise me."

"So what you're saying is that wasn't a hit?"

"Well since you asked Detective you must not know, which you leave me surprised. Once again, I thought you knew what was going on."

"I thought I knew a lot, I guess I will hear it from directly from the horse's mouth now."

"Well let me just tell you this the man that died in that car needed to die. I was tired of living a double life, living a lie. Take a look at me this I'm living the life I always wanted to live."

After talking he paused and pulled out a knot of Benjamin's from his pants pockets then continued.

"See this? I was tired of pretending to be something I'm not, and from the sight of this power I hold in my hand this is where I need to be. I'm not gone lie, I was power tripping still when I was living the lie out, but now I feel even more fulfilled now that's over with."

After speaking he put his knot back into his pocket and took a puff from his cigarette.

"So you staged your own death. How long did it take you to plan that?"

The culprit blew out his smoke while laughing at Detective Patterson's question. He then gained his composure before he answered.

"Plan? This wasn't a wedding Detective, people plan weddings. This was a master plan. My actions lead me thus far."

After answering the questions, there were thirty seconds of dead silence in the room as Detective Patterson was going over all the info he had and all the info he was receiving. It was a little overwhelming to take in that he participated in a funeral that had no body in the coffin. And to add to that the person that was supposed to be in the coffin he was having a conversation with in his living room.

"So give me this much Frank. You were behind all the chaos between the Jamaicans and the Gwap Gang, right?"

"Hell yeah. I orchestrated the whole thing, and it worked out quite well. The plan, as they say, was well-executed."

"So Frank... what happens from here? I mean, do we remain enemies?"

Frank Moretti let out a sly snicker then answered the question.

"Enemies. Whoever said that we were enemies in the first place? I never looked at you as my enemy. Me and you lead two different lives. Oh let me tell you the feeling I got fucking somebody else's wife. Wow, what a feeling! I see why you do it now. But look Detective this conversation is now over. You're going to let me walk out of here and we will go our separate ways."

"So I'm supposed to let you just walk out of here without being arrested and calling you in."

"What you gone say, detective? Frank's sitting in my living room. I'm dead, detective! Who's going to believe you after I have been buried? Let me stay dead at least until I feel it's necessary to either show my face or make it known. Oh and one more thing before I leave, I just wanted to let you know your Captain... he's no angel. Believe me. I should know."

Frank stood up fixed his suit jacket and walked pass Detective Patterson without the Detective laying a single finger on him. He exited Detective's Patterson's condo as smooth as he entered. Detective Patterson just sat down on his couch and exhaled and begin to think about the last words Frank Moretti left him with.

* * * * *

It was 2 a.m. and the club was still packed from another successful Gwap Gang show. It was genius for them to make the show a live recording this made every female in the city want to come and show love so they can get a once in a lifetime chance to be in the Gwap Gang video. During the show, Benji stepped out to see how turnout was and it bought a smile to his face to see how packed his club was. He decided that he would give them their own day at his club since they were so successful tonight. Benji knew this was a move he needed to make if he wanted to open another club. After all the dudes and the groupies spilled into the parking lot all the dancers that were live on stage went into the dressing room to get dressed. Some groupies were trying to stick around to leave with the Gwap Gang but Benji's security kicked them out into the parking lot. Chase and the rest of the crew were busy waiting for the dancers they had on stage minus Erica and Janine. Once the dancers were ready they decided to exit and hit the crib for their own private after party. Before they could leave Benji caught up to Chase Money and the rest of the crew so they could go back to his office to discuss business. Banks, Scrilla, and Paperboi decided to skip the meeting to linger in the parking lot before all the groupies left to collect phone numbers.

"Listen you guys did the dam thing tonight! I want to give you guys your own night at my club. I just need to know how much that's gone take."

"How about you give us the door and you don't have to pay us?" Chase Money said negotiating with Benji.

"How bout I give up half of the door and 10% of the bar?" Benji said not willing to give up the door.

"Cool you got deal Benji," Chase said sticking out his hand for a handshake.

"Oh and before you leave here's half of the door," Benji said then taking it back.

"Hold up since I see you guys leaving with some of my girls I have to take off $500 from this $2,500 I was gone pass off to you."

"Damn. I see why they call you Benji."

"Oh yeah. I'm about my business 24/7," Benji said putting the extra hundreds in his pocket.

"Cool so we are done here. Now make sure you guys take extra care of my girls," Benji said as he got up to let everybody out of his office.

As soon as he rose one of his security came running in to tell him that his parking lot turned into the World War 2.

"Hey Benji. Something jumped off in the parking lot had to call the cops man."

"What the fuck happened?" Benji yelled as he ran out of his office.

Chase Money and Stacks was right behind him knowing that Banks, Paperboi and Scrilla were in the parking lot. As they ran to see what was going on a couple of more shots rang out.

"Aww shit! They shooting up my parking lot! Goddamnit!" Benji yelled out as he ducked down in the front door booth.

Chase Money and Stacks made it to the front where they found the front door shattered from the shootout. Chase Money pulled out his cell phone to hit up Banks to make sure they were cool.

"Yo Banks where the fuck y'all at?" Chase said as Banks answered.

"We had to bounce my nigga. We ran into that nigga Rizz while we were parking lot pimpin'. Of course it was on sight with them niggas from what happened at Danny Wok so they pulled out and tried to merk us my nigga. Couple of bitches that we was hollering at got hit trying to run away hopefully ain't nobody get killed."

"Oh shit! Did anyone of y'all get hit up?" Chase asked hoping that his niggas was cool.

"We got away clean. If it wasn't for that crowd then I think we would have got hit," Banks said.

"Cool my nigga I will meet y'all around the way," Chase said as he hung up.

Chase let out his frustrations as soon as he hung up the phone knowing that this was gone fuck his business transaction that just went down.

Fuck!

"Where them niggas at?" Stacks asked.

"Them niggas got shot at in the parking lot Stacks, and a Banks said a couple of people got shot," Chase explained.

The cops arrived with ambulances and shut the parking lot down completely. They started their investigation pulling Benji Stacks and Chase Money inside. Even pulling his security to the side. It was a couple of females getting questioned crying frantically from being caught up in the shootout. The ones with the girlfriends that were put inside the ambulances followed them to the hospital.

* * * * *

Erica woke up with her whole body sore from all the ass shaking she did from being on the stage with Gwap Gang. After going to the bathroom, washing her face and brushing her teeth she lay back down and turned on her TV. She picked up her phone and noticed that she had five missed calls.

"Damn I must have been knocked out," Erica said out loud.

One call was from Mr. Hard she was about to call until the news caught her attention.

"Shootout last night left five shot left in stable condition, and seven people injured. Club is being investigated and is temporarily shut down until investigation is complete".

"Oh shit," Erica thought as she turned off the TV.

Erica began to think about what she was going do while the club was closed. She thought about and used this incident as way to get away. She grabbed her cell phone and called the one person that wouldn't mind having her for company for a while until everything got back to normal.

* * * * *

Bishop Williams pulled up to the Philadelphia International Airport.

"What company you flying with Erica again?" Bishop Williams asked.

"AirTran, Dad. I told you like five times already," Erica answered sounding a little irritated.

"Well how about I don't want you to go, you just gone up and leave me and Dawud here."

"Listen Dad I'm not flying out to L.A to stay its only temporary until the club situation blows over."

"Well you could've stayed and worked for me."

"Look Dad you drove me all the way to the airport to argue about me leaving, look I got a plane to catch can you please grab my bag from trunk," Erica said as she got out of the car.

Erica opened the backdoor to give Dawud a hug and kiss.

"Come here baby and give mommy a hug and kiss, and you better be good for your grandpop."

"I will Mommy," Dawud said in an innocent kid voice.

"Good that's what mommy wants to hear," Erica said as she hugged her little prince and gave him a tight hug.

"Thanks for getting my bag, Dad. Now I know I don't need to tell you to be good Bishop,"

Bishop chuckled at his daughter words and gave her a hug.

"Listen here when you land make sure you call so I know you made it in one piece, and please while you're out there take good care of yourself."

"I sure will Daddy," Erica said as she grabbed her luggage and walked inside the airport directly to check in.

She went through the proper protocol as far as showing her ticket, going through security bag check and making it to the boarding area. Erica was always nervous about getting on planes so she went straight to a bar before it was time to board. She sat down and ordered a Southern Comfort and ginger ale. By the time she finished they were calling her to board. She was nice and tipsy not even feeling an ounce of nervousness when she boarded. She just sat down in her window seat waited till the stewardess went through the video about all the safety precautions. The light finally came on signaling the plane to fasten their seatbelts and then began to move towards take off position. Shortly thereafter, the plane was taking off and Erica's trip to L.A began. She just enjoyed the view out of the window as the plane rose in altitude. Once the plane reached maximum altitude, she asked the flight attendant for a blanket and pillow so she could get some sleep.

"L.A. here I come!" Erica exclaimed, exhaled, and then closed her eyes.

To be continued…

T. Real – Biography

Terrell Jones (Author T. Real) is a multifaceted person with credits under his belt that include author, playwright, graphic tee designer and entrepreneur. Born in Texas and being able to travel as a child, he found his own creativity through writing with influences from fiction greats like Donald Goines, Omar Tyree, Michael Baisden and Sistah Souljah. His vision proved to be outside the box and from life experiences a creative soul was born.

After signing his first publishing deal with Johnson Publications, Terrell went on to release his debut novel, *Homicide City*, and the later titles

Bitter Sweet and *Cocktales*. Recognized for his writing ability he was also a contributing author for the reader's favorite anthology, *Erotic Snapshots* presented by Essence best-selling author, Anna J.

Wanting to have more control of his literary fate, Terrell launched his own publishing company, Made Man Inc. and through this imprint he released *Cousin of Death* and upcoming works which include the sequel to his debut novel as well as the production of *Right Man Wrong Time,* a play based off of the novel of the same name and the release of his graphic tee line.

Currently, Terrell is a proud father who resides in Philadelphia who continues to create while leaving a legacy.

Connect with T. Real

Facebook.com/AuthorT.Real
Twitter: @trealdaauthor
Instagram: @trealdaauthor

31905514R10142

Made in the USA
Middletown, DE
18 May 2016